Dard Nordis grew up in a world that had been devastated by atomic catastrophe. The remnants of humanity had set up an iron dictatorship to hunt out and destroy the last free bands of scientists, hiding in mountains and caves. And the day came when Dard's secret laboratory home was raided—and he escaped by the skin of his teeth.

Where else could men go to keep the torch of liberty and knowledge burning? Dard's martyred brother had given him a key to the unknown haven, but how could Dard learn to use it? Where were the engineers and their spaceships hidden?

The gripping, always exciting story of how Dard Nordis fought his way through an antagonistic world to find the gateway to the stars is one of Andre Norton's finest science-fiction novels.

ANDRE NORTON

THE STARS ARE OURS!

SF

ace books

A Division of Charter Communications Inc.
A GROSSET & DUNLAP COMPANY
51 Madison Avenue
New York, New York 10010

THE STARS ARE OURS!

For HARLAN ELLISON

Who is a veteran of galactic voyages and an ever

prepared guide to the realms of outer Space

This Ace Printing: September 1981
Printed in U.S.A.
Printed simultaneously in Canada

BOOK ONE

TERRA

PROLOGUE

(Except from the Encyclopedia Galactica)

THE FIRST GALACTIC exploratory and colonization flight came as a direct outgrowth of a peculiar sociological-political situation on the planet Terra. As a result of a series of wars between nationalistic divisions atomic power was discovered. Afraid of the demon they had so loosed the nations then engaged in so-called "cold wars" during which all countries raced to outbuild each other in the stock piling of new and more drastic weapons and the mobilization of manpower into the ancient "armies."

Scientific training became valued only for the aid it could render in helping to arm and fit a nation for war. For some time scientists and techneers of all classes were kept in a form of peonage by "security" regulations. But a unification of scientists fostered in a secret underground movement resulted in the formation of "Free Scientist" teams, groups of experts and specialists who sold their services to both private industry and governments as research workers. Since they gave no attention to the racial, political, or religious antecedents of their members, they became truly international and planet-, instead of nation-, minded—a situation both hated and feared by their employers.

Under the stimulus of Free Scientist encouragement man

achieved interplanetary flight. Terra was the third in a series of nine planets revolving about the sun, Sol I. It possessed one satellite, Luna.

Exploration ships made landings on Luna, and the two neighboring planets, Mars and Venus. None of these worlds were suitable for human colonization without vast expenditure, and they offered little or no return for such effort. Consequently, after the first flurry of interest, space flight died down, and there were few visitors to the other worlds, except for the purpose of research.

Three "space stations" had been constructed to serve Terra as artificial satellites. These were used for refueling interplanetary ships and astronomical and meteorological observation. One of these provided the weapon the nationalists had been searching for in their war against the "Free Scientists."

The station was invaded and occupied by a party of unidentified armed men (later studies suggest that these men were mercenaries in the pay of nationalist forces). And this group, either by ignorant chance or with deliberate purpose, turned certain installations in the station into weapons for an attack upon Terra. There are indications that they themselves had no idea of the power they unleashed, and that it was at once beyond their control.

As a result the major portion of the thickly populated sections of the planet were completely devastated and no one was ever able to reckon the loss of life.

Among those who were the sole survivors of an entire family group was Arturo Renzi. Renzi, a man of unusual magnetic personality, was a believer in narrow and fanatical nationalist doctrines. Because of his personal loss he began to preach the evil of science (with propaganda that the Free Scientists themselves had turned the station against the earth that had apparently been carefully prepared even before the act) and the necessity for man to return to the simple life on the soil to save himself and Terra.

To a people already in psychic shock from the enormity of the disaster, Renzi appeared the great leader they needed and his party came into power around the world.

But, fanatic and narrow as he was, his voiced policies were still too liberal for some of his supporters.

Renzi's assassination, an act committed by a man arbitrarily identified as an outlawed Free Scientist, touched off the terrible purge which lasted three days. At the end of which time the few scientists and techneers still alive had been driven into hiding, to be hunted down one by one through the following years as chance or man betrayed them.

Saxon Bort, a lieutenant of Renzi's, assumed command of the leader's forces and organized the tight dictatorship of the Company of Pax.

Learning, unless one was a privileged "Peaceman," became suspect. Society was formed into three classes, the nobility as represented by the Peacemen of various grades, the peasantry on the land, and the work-slaves—descendants of suspected scientists or techneers.

With the stranglehold of Pax firmly established on Terra, old prejudices against different racial and religious origins again developed. All research, invention, and study was proscribed and the planet was fast slipping into an age of total darkness and retreat. Yet it was at this moment in her history that the first galactic flight was made.

SEE ALSO:

Astra: First Colony
Free Scientists
Renzi, Arturo
Terra: Space Flight

1. THE ROUNDUP

DARD NORDIS PAUSED beneath the low-hanging branches
of a pine, sheltered for the moment from the worst of the
cutting wind. The western sky was striped with color,
dusky purple, gold, red almost as sultry as if this were
August instead of late November. But for all their splen-
dor the colors were as bleakly chill as the wind whipping
his too-thin body through the sleazy rags of clothing.

He shrugged his shoulders, trying to settle more evenly
the bundle of firewood which bowed him into an old man.
There came a tug at the hide thong serving him as a belt.

"Dard—there's an animal watching—over there—"

He stiffened. To Dessie, with her odd kinship for all
furred creatures, every animal was a friend. She might now
be speaking of a squirrel or—a wolf! He looked down to the
smaller, ragged figure beside him and moistened suddenly dry lips.

"Is it a big one?" he asked.

Hands, which wrappings of sackcloth made into shapeless paws, projected to measure off slightly more than a foot
of air.

"So big. I think it's a fox—it must be cold. Could we—
could we take it home?" Those eyes, which seemed to fill
about a quarter of the grimy little face turned up to his,
were wistful as well as filled with a too-old patience.

He shook his head. "Foxes have thick fur skins—they're
warmer than we are, honey. He probably has a home and

8

is going there now. Think you can pull the wood all the way down to the path?"

Her mouth twisted in an indignant pout. " 'Course. I'm not a baby any more. It's awfully cold, though, isn't it, Dardie? Wish it were summer again."

She gave a quick jerk on a piece of hide and brought into grudging motion the flat piece of battered wood which served as a sled. It was piled high with branches and a few pieces of shredded bark. Not much of a haul today, even combining Dessie's bits and patches with his own load. But since their axe had vanished it was the best they could do.

He followed the little girl down the slope, retracing the tracks they had made two hours before. There was a frown drawing deep lines between his black brows. That axe—it hadn't just been mislaid—it had been stolen. By whom? By someone who knew just what its loss would mean, who wanted to cripple them. And that would be Hew Folley. But Hew had not been near the farm for weeks—or had he—secretly?

If he could only get Lars to see that Folley was a danger. Folley was a landsman which made him a fanatic servant of Pax. The once independent farmers had always believed in peace—true peace not the iron stagnation imposed by Pax—and they had early been won over as firm followers of Renzi. When their sturdy independence had been entirely swallowed up by the strangle controls of those who had assumed command after the death of the Prophet, some had rebelled—too late. Landsmen were now as proud of their lack of education as they were retentive of the few favors allowed them. And it was from their ranks the hated Peacemen were recruited.

Folley was a fervid follower of Pax and for a long time he had wanted to add the few poor Nordis acres to his own holding. If he ever came to suspect their descent—that they were of Free Scientist blood! If he ever guessed what Lars was doing even now!

"Dardie, why must we run?"

Dard caught his breath in a half sob and slowed. That prick of frantic panic which had sent him plunging down to the main trail still goaded him. It was always this way when he was away from the farm even for an hour or two. Each time he feared to return to . . . Resolutely he closed his mind to the picture his imagination was only too ready to supply him. He forced his lips into a set half-smile for Dessie's sake.

"Going to be dark early tonight, Dessie. See those big clouds?"

"Snow, Dardie?"

"Probably. We'll be glad to have this wood."

"I hope that the fox gets home to his den before the snow comes. He will, won't he?"

"Of course he will. We'd better, too. Let's try to run, Dessie—here along the trail—"

She regarded doubtfully the almost shapeless blobs of wrappings which concealed her feet. "My feet don't run very well, Dardie. Too many coverings on them, maybe. And they're cold now—"

Not frostbite—not frostbite! he prayed. They had been lucky so far. Of course they were always cold, and very often hungry. But they had had no accidents, nor serious illnesses.

"Run!" he commanded sharply, and Dessie's short-legged shuffle became a trot.

But, when they reached the screen of second-growth brush at the end of the north field, she halted in obedience to old orders. Dard shrugged off the bundle of firewood and dropped to his hands and knees, crawling forward under cover until he could look down across the broken field-stone wall to the house.

Carefully he examined the sweep of snow about the half-ruined dwelling. There were the tracks he and Dessie had made about the yard. But the smooth expanse of white between house and main road was unbroken. There had been no invaders since they had left. Thankfully, though without any lessening of his habitual apprehension, he went back to gather up the wood.

"All right?" Dessie shifted impatiently from one cold foot to the other.

"All right."

She jerked the sled into motion and plodded on along the wall where the snow had not drifted. There was a faint gleam of light in one of the windows below. Lars must be in the kitchen. Minutes later they stamped off snow and went in.

Lars Nordis raised his head as his daughter and then his brother entered. His smile of welcome was hardly more than a stretch of parchment skin over thrusting bones and Dard's secret fear deepened as he studied Lars anxiously. They were always hungry, but tonight Lars had the appearance of a man in the last stages of starvation.

"Good haul?" he asked Dard as the boy began to shed his first layer of the sacking which served him as a coat.

"Good as we could do without the axe. Dessie got a lot of pine cones."

Lars swung around to his daughter who had squatted down before the small fire on the hearth where she began to methodically unwind the strips of burlap which were her mittens.

"Now that was lucky! Did you see anything interesting, Dessie?" He spoke to her as he might have addressed an adult.

"Just a fox," she reported gravely. "It was watching us—from under a tree. It looked cold—but Dardie said it had a home—"

"So it did, honey," Lars assured her. "A little cave or a hollow tree."

"I wish I could have brought it home. It would be nice to have a fox or a squirrel—or something—to live with us." She stretched her small, grime-encrusted, chapped hands out to the fire.

"Maybe someday . . ." Lars' voice trailed off. He stared across Dessie's head at the scanty flames.

Dard hung up the cobbled mass of tatters which was his outdoor coat and went to the cupboard. He lifted

11

down an unwholesome block of salted meat as his brother spoke again.

"How are supplies?"

Dard tensed. There was more to that question than was merely routine. He surveyed the pitiful array on the shelves jealously.

"How much?" he asked, unable to keep out of his voice the almost despairing resentment he felt.

"Maybe enough for two days—if you can put up such a packet."

Swiftly Dard's eyes measured and portioned. "If it is really necessary—" he couldn't stop that half-protest. This systematic robbing of their own, too scanty hoard—for what? If Lars would only explain! But he knew Lars' answer to that, too: The less one knew, the better, these days. Even in a family that could be so. All right, he'd make up that packet of food and leave it here on the table and in the morning it would be gone—given to someone he didn't know and would never see. And within a week, or maybe a month it would happen again. . . .

"Tonight?" He asked only that as he sawed away at the wood-like meat.

"I don't know."

And at the tone of his brother's answer Dard dropped the dull knife to turn and watch Lars' face. There was a new light in the man's eyes, a brightness about him that his younger brother had never seen since Dessie's mother had died two years before.

"You've finished," Dard said slowly, hardly daring to believe what might be true, that they might be free!

"I've finished. They'll pass the word and then we'll be sent for."

"Honey," Dard called to Dessie, "bring in the pine cones. We'll have a big fire tonight."

As she scampered toward the shed Dard spoke over her head.

"There's a heavy snow on the way, Lars."

"So?" the man at the table did not appear worried.

"Well, snow's never stopped them from coming before."
He was relaxed, at peace.

Dard was silent but his eyes flickered beyond Lars' shoulder to the objects leaning against the wall. They were never mentioned, those crutches. But in deep snow! Lars never went outside in winter, he couldn't! How could they get away unless the mysterious others had a horse or horses. But perhaps they did. That was always his greatest fault—worrying over the future—borrowing trouble ahead, as if they didn't have enough already to go around!

Dessie was back to feed the fire slowly one cone at a time. Dard scraped the meat slivers into the iron pot and added a shriveled potato carefully diced. Then he grew reckless and wrenched off the lid of a can to pour its treasured contents to thicken the water. If they were going away they'd need feeding up to make the trip and there would be little sense in hoarding supplies they could not carry with them.

"Birthday?" Dessie watched this move in wide-eyed surprise. "But my birthday's in the summer, and Daddy's was last month, and yours," she counted on her fingers, "is not for a long time yet, Dardie."

"Not a birthday. Just a celebration. Get the spoon, Dessie, and stir this carefully."

"Celebration," she considered the new word thoughtfully. "I like celebrations. You going to make tea, too, Dardie? Why, this is just like a birthday!"

Dard shook the dried leaves out on the palm of his hand. Their aromatic fragrance reached him faintly. Mint, green and cool under the sun. He sensed that he was different from Lars—colors, scents, certain sounds meant more to him. Just as Dessie was different in her way—in her ability to make friends with birds and animals. He had seen her last summer, sitting perfectly still on the wall, two birds on her shoulders and a squirrel nuzzling her hand.

But Lars had gifts, too. Only he had been taught to use them. Dard shook the last crumbling leaf from his hand into the pot and wondered for the thousandth time what it would have been like to live in the old days when the Free Scientists had the right to teach and learn and experiment. It probably had been another kind of world altogether—the one which existed before the Big Burning, before Renzi had preached the Great Peace.

All he could remember of his early childhood in those days was a vague happiness. The purge had come when he was eight and Lars twenty-five, and after that things simply got worse and worse. Of course, they'd been lucky to survive the purge at all—belonging to a Scientific family. But their escape had left Lars a twisted cripple. He and Lars and Kathia had come here. But Kathia was different—she forgot everything, mercifully. And after Dessie had been born five months later it had been like caring for two babies at once. Kathia had been sweet and obedient and lovely, but she lived in her own dream world and neither of them had ever tried to bring her out of it. Seven, almost eight years now, they had been here. But in all that time Dard had never quite dared to believe they were safe. He lived always on the ragged edge of fear. Maybe Kathia had been the luckiest one of all.

He took over the stirring of the stew and Dessie set the table, putting out the three wooden spoons, the battered crockery bowl, the tin basin and the single chipped soup dish, the two tin cups and the graceful fluted china one, which had been Dessie's last birthday gift after he had found it hidden on a rafter out in the barn.

"Smells grand, Dard. You're a good cook, son." Lars offered praise.

Dessie bobbed her head in agreement until her two pencil-thick braids flopped up and down on shoulders where the blades, as she moved, took on the angular outlines of wings. "I like celebrations!" She announced. "Tonight may we play the word game?"

"We certainly shall!" Lars returned with emphatic promptness.

Dard did not pause in his stirring though he was alert to every inflection in Lars' voice. Did he read a special

14

significance into that last answer? Why did Lars want to play the word game? And why did he himself feel this aroused wariness—as if they were secure in a den while out in the dark danger prowled!

"I have a new one," Dessie went on, "It sings—"

She put her hands down on the table on either side of her soup plate and tapped her little broken nails in time to the words she recited:

> "Eesee, Osee, Icksee, Ann,
> Fullson, Follson, Orson, Cann."

Dard made an effort and pushed the rhythm out of his mind—no time now to "see" the pattern in that. Why did he always "see" words mentally arranged in the up and down patterns of lines? That was as much a part of him as his delight in color, texture, sight and sound. And for the past three years Lars had encouraged him to work upon it, setting him problems of stray lines of old poetry.

"Yes, that sings, Dessie," Lars was agreeing now. "I heard you humming it this morning. And there is a reason why Dard must make us a pattern—" he broke off abruptly and Dard did not try to question him.

They ate silently, ladling the hot stuff into them, lifting the dishes to drink the last drops. But they lingered over the spicy mint drink, feeling its warmth sink into their starved, chilled bodies. The light given out by the fire was meager; only now and again did it reach Lars' face, and shadows were thick in the corners of the room. Dard made no move to light the greased fagot supported by the iron loop above the table. He was too tired and listless. But Dessie rounded the table and leaned against Lars' crooked shoulder.

"You promised—the word game," she reminded him.

"Yes—the game—"

With a sigh Dard stooped to pick up a charred stick from the hearth. But he was sure now about the suppressed excitement in his brother's voice. With the blackened wood for a pencil and the table top for his writing pad he waited.

"Suppose we try your verse now, Dessie," Lars suggested. "Repeat it slowly so Dard can work out the pattern."

Dard's stick moved in a series of lines up, down, up again. It made a pattern right enough and a clear one. Dessie came to look and then she laughed.

"Legs kicking, Daddy. My rhyme make a picture of legs kicking!"

Dard studied what he had just done. Dessie was right, legs kicked, one a little more exuberantly than the other. He smiled and then glanced up with a start, for Lars had struggled to his feet and was edging around the table without the aid of his crutches. He looked at the straggling lines, his brows drawn together in a frown of concentration. From the breast pocket of his patched shirt he took out a scrap of peeled bark they used for paper—keeping it half-concealed in the palm of his hand so that what was noted on it remained a secret. Taking the writing stick from Dard he began to make notations, but the scratchings were all numbers not words.

Erasing with the side of his hand now and again he worked feverishly until at last he gave a quick nod as if in self-reassurance, and let his last combinations stand among the line pattern Dard had seen in Dessie's nonsense rhyme.

"This is important—both of you—" his voice was almost a whip lash of impatient command. "The pattern you see for Dessie's lines, Dard—but—these words." Slowly he recited, accenting heavily each word he spoke.

"Seven, nine, four and ten.
Twenty, sixty, and seven again."

Dard studied the smudged diagram on the table top until he was sure that it was engraved on his memory for all time.

When he nodded, Lars turned and tossed the note chip into the fire. Then his eyes met his brother's in a straight measuring look over the little girl's bent head.

"It's all yours, Dard, just remember—"

But the younger Nordis had only said, "I'll do it," when Dessie, uncomprehendingly, broke in.

"Seven, nine, four and ten," she repeated solemnly.

"Twenty, sixty, and seven again. Why, it sings just as mine does—you're right, Daddy!"

"Yes. Now how about bed." Lars lurched back to his chair. "It's dark. You'd better go, too, Dard."

That was an order. Lars was expecting someone tonight, then. Dard raked two bricks away from the fire and wrapped them up in charred pieces of blanket. Then he opened the door to the crooked stairs which led to the room overhead. There it was dark and the cold was bitter. But moonlight made a short path from the uncurtained window— enough to show them the pile of straw and ragged bed covers huddled close to the chimney where some heat came up from the fire below. Dard made a nest with the bricks laid in to warm it and pushed Dessie back as far as he could without smothering her. Then he stood for a moment looking out across the moonlit snow.

They were a safe mile from the road and he had taken certain precautions of his own to insure that no sneaking patrol of Peacemen could enter the lane without warning. Across the fields was only Folley's place—though that was a lurking danger. Behind loomed the mountains, which, wild as they were, promised safety of a kind. If only Lars were not crippled they could have gone into the hills long ago.

When they first reached the farm it had seemed a haven of safety after two years of hiding and being hunted. There was so much confusion after Renzi's assassination and the following purge, with the Peacemen busily consolidating their power, that small fry among the remaining techneers and scientists had managed to stay free of the first nets. But now patrols were combing everywhere and some day, sooner or later, one would come here—especially if Folley revealed his suspicions to the right people. Folley wanted the farm, and he hated Lars and Dard because they were different. To be different nowadays was to sign your own death warrant. How much longer *would* they escape the notice of a roundup gang?

Dard was aroused from the blackest of forebodings to

discover that he was biting savagely on the knuckles of a
balled fist. With two quick steps he crossed the small
room and felt along the shelf. His heart leaped as his
groping fingers closed about the haft of a knife. Not much
good against a stun rifle maybe. But when he held it so,
he did not feel completely defenseless.

On impulse he put it inside his clothing, against skin
which shrunk from the icy metal. And then he crawled
into the nest of straw.

"Hmm—?" came a sleepy murmur from Dessie.

"It's Dardie," he whispered reassuringly. "Go to sleep."

It might have been hours later, or minutes, when Dard
came suddenly awake. He lay rigid, listening. There was
no sound in the old house, not even the creak of a board.
But he pulled out into the cold and crawled to the window. Something had awakened him, and the fear he lived
with put him on guard.

He strained to see all the details of the bright white
and black landscape. A shadow moved between moon
and snow. There was a 'copter coming down, making a silent landing just before the house. Figures leaped out of
it and flitted to right and left, encircling the dwelling.

Dard ran back to scoop Dessie out of the warmth of
the bed, clapping his hand over her mouth. Her eyes
opened, wide with fear, as he put his lips close to her ear.

"Go down to Daddy," he ordered. "Wake him."

"Peacemen?" She was shaking with more than cold as
she started down the stairs.

"Say that I think so. They came in a 'copter." That was
the one thing he had not been able to guard against—
surprise from above. But they had so few of the 'copters
left, now that it was forbidden to manufacture any of
the prepurge machines. And why should they use one to
raid an insignificant farmhouse sheltering a child, a cripple and a boy? Unless Lars' work was important—so important that they dared not allow him to pass along his findings to the underground.

Dard watched the dark shapes take cover. They were

probably all around the house by this time, moving in. They wanted to take the inhabitants alive. Too many cornered scientists in the past had cheated them. So they would move slowly now—slow enough to—Dard's smile was no more than a drawn grimace. He still had one secret, one which might save the Nordis family yet.

Having watched the last of the raiders take cover, Dard ran down into the kitchen. The fire was still burning, and before it crouched Lars.

"They came by air. And they have the house surrounded," Dard reported in a matter-of-fact voice. Now that the worst had at last happened he was surprisingly calm. "But they don't have their trap completely closed—as they are going to discover!"

He brushed past Lars and jerked open the cupboard doors. Dessie stood beside her father, and now Dard threw her a bag.

"Food—everything you can pack in," he ordered. "Lars, here!"

From the pegs he pulled down all the extra clothing they had. "Get dressed to go out."

But his brother shook his head. "You know I can't make it, Dard."

Dessie went on stuffing provisions into the bag. "I'll help you, Daddy," she promised, "just as soon as I can."

Dard paid no attention to his brother. Instead he ran to the far end of the room and raised the trap door of the cellar.

"Last summer," he explained as he came back to gather up the clothing, "I found a passage down there, behind the wall. It leads out to the foundations of the barn. We can hide there—"

"They know we are here. They'll be looking for a move such as that," objected Lars.

"Not after I cover our trail."

He saw that Lars was pulling on the remnants of a coat. Dessie was almost ready to go and now she helped her father not only to dress but to crawl across the floor to the hole. Dard gave her a pine knot torch before he went to work.

The doors and all the downstairs shutters were barred. Those ought to hold just long enough—

He took a small can from the cupboard and poured its long-saved contents liberally about the room. Then he withdrew to the head of the cellar ladder before hurling a second blazing torch into the nearest patch of liquid. A billow of fire sent him hurtling down with just enough time to pull the trap door shut behind him.

As he shoved aside the rotting bins which concealed the opening to the passage, he could hear the crackling above, and smoke drifted down through the flooring cracks.

A moment later Dessie scuttled into the passage ahead as Dard hauled Lars along with him. Over their heads the house burned. These outside might well believe that their prey burned with it. At the very least the blaze would cover their escape for the precious minutes which meant the difference between life and death.

2. HIDING OUT

BEFORE THEY REACHED the outlet below the barn, Dard brought them to a halt. There was no use emerging into the arms of some snooping Peaceman. It was better to stay in hiding until they could see whether or not the enemy had been fooled by the burning house.

The passage in which the three crouched was walled with rough stone and so narrow that the shoulders of the two adults brushed both sides. It was cold, icy with a chill which crept up from the bare earth underneath through their ill-covered feet to their knees and then into their shivering bodies. How long they could stay there without succumbing to that cold Dard did not know. He bit his lip anxiously as he strained to hear the sound from above.

He was answered by an explosion, the sound and shock of which came to them down the passage from the house. And then there was a slightly hysterical chuckle from Lars.

"What happened?" began Dard, and then answered his own question, "The laboratory!"

"Yes, the laboratory," Lars said, leaning against the wall. There was relaxation in both his pose and voice. "They'll have a mess to comb through now."

"All the better!" snapped Dard. "Will it feed the fire?"

"Feed the fire! It might blow up the whole building. There won't be enough pieces left for them to discover what was inside before the blast."

"Or who might have been there!" For the first time Dard saw a ray of real hope. The Peacemen could not have known of this passage, they probably believed that the dwellers in the farmhouse had been blown up in that explosion. The escape of the Nordis family was covered—they now had a better than even chance.

But still he waited, or rather made Lars and Dessie wait in hiding while he crept on into the barn hole and climbed up the ladder he had placed there for such a use as this. Then, making a worm's progress crawling, he crossed the rotting floor to peer out through the doorless entrance.

The outline of the farmhouse walls was gone, and tongues of blue-white flame ate up the dark to make the scene daybright. Two men in the black and white Peace uniforms were dragging a third away from the holocaust. And there was a lot of confused shouting. Dard listened and gathered that the raiders were convinced that their prey had gone up with the house, taking with them two officers who had just beaten in the back door before the explo-

21

sion. And there had been three others injured. The round up gang was hurrying away, apprehensive of other explosions. Peacemen, who prided themselves on their lack of scientific knowledge, were apt to harbor such suspicions.

Dard got to his feet. The last man, trailing a stun rifle, was going around the fire now, keeping a careful distance from the chemically fed flames, such a distance that he plunged waist deep through snow drifts. And a few moments later Dard saw the 'copter rise, circle the farm once, and head west. He sighed with relief and went back to get the others.

"All clear," he reported to Lars as he supported the crippled man up the ladder. "They think we went up in the explosion and they were afraid there might be another so they left fast——"

Again Lars chuckled. "They won't be back in a hurry then."

"Dard," Dessie was a small shadow moving through the gloom, "if our house is gone where are we going to live now?"

"My practical daughter," Lars said. "We will find some other place. . . ."

Dard remembered. "The messenger you were expecting! He might see the blaze from the hills and not come at all!"

"And that's why you're going to leave him a sign that we're still in the land of the living, Dard. As Dessie points out we haven't a roof over us now, and the sooner we're on our way the better. Since our late callers believe us to be dead there's no danger in Dessie and I staying right where we are now, while you do what's necessary to bring help. Follow the wall in the top pasture to the corner where the old woods road begins. About a quarter of a mile beyond is a big tree with a hollow in it. Put this inside." Lars pulled a piece of rag out of his wrappings. "Then come back here. That'll bring our man on down even if he sees an eruption going on. It tells him that we've escaped and are hiding out waiting to make contact.

f he doesn't come by morning—we'll try moving up closer
o the tree."

Dard understood. His brother daren't attempt the journey through the snow and brush at night. But tomorrow
they could rig some kind of a board sled from the debris
and drag Lars into the safety of the woods. In the meantime it was very necessary to leave the sign. With a word
of caution to them both, Dard left the barn.

By instinct he kept to the shadows cast by the trees
and brush which encroached on the once fertile fields. Near
the farm buildings was a maze of tracks left by the Peacemen, and he used them to hide the pattern of his own
steps. Just why he took such precautions he could not tell,
but the wariness which had guided every move of his life
for years had now become an ingrown part of him. On
the other hand, now that the raid he had feared for so
long had come, and he and his were still alive and free,
he felt eased of some of the almost intolerable burden.

As he tramped away from the dying fire the night was
very still and cold. Once a snowy owl slipped across the
sky, and deep in the forest a wolf, or one of the predatory
wild dogs, howled. Dard did not find it difficult to locate Lars' tree and made sure that the rag was safe in
the black hollow of its trunk.

The cold ate into him and he hurried on his back trail.
Maybe they might dare light a small fire in the cellar
pit, just enough to keep them from freezing until morning. How close was the dawn, he wondered, as he stumbled and clutched at a snow-crowned wall to steady himself. Bed—sleep—warmth—— He was so tired—so very tired

Then a sound ripped through the night air. A shot! His
face twisted and his hand went to the haft of the knife.
A shot! Lars had no gun! The Peacemen—but they had
gone!

Clumsily, slipping, fighting to keep his footing in the
treacherous snow drifts, Dard began to run. Within a
matter of minutes he came to his senses and dodged into

cover, making his way to the barn in such a manner as to provide no target for any marksman lurking there. Dessie, Lars—there alone without any means of defense!

Dard was close to he building when Dessie's scream came. And that scream tore all the caution from him. Balancing the knife in his hand, he threw himself across the churned snow of the yard for the door. And his sacking covered feet made no sound as he ran.

"Got ya'—imp of Satan!"

Dard's arm came up, the knife was poised. And, as if for once Fortune was on his side, there was a sharp tinkle of breaking glass from the embers of the house and a following sweep of flame to light the scene within the barn.

Dessie was fighting, silently now, with all the frenzy of a small cornered animal, in the hands of Hew Folley. One of the man's hard fists was aimed straight for her face as Dard threw the knife.

The months he had practiced with that single weapon were now rewarded. Dessie flew free as the man hurled her away. On hands and feet she scuttled into the dark. Hew turned and bent over as if to grope for the rifle which lay by his feet. Then he coughed, and coughing, went down. Dard grabbed the rifle. Only when it was in his hands did he come up to the still-coughing man. He pulled at Folley's shoulder and rolled him over. Bitter hatred stared up at Dard from the small dark eyes of the other.

"Got—dirty—stinkman——" Folley mouthed and then coughed. Blood bubbled from his slack lips. "Thought—he —was—hiding—right—— Kill—kill——" The rest was lost in a gush of blood. He tried to raise himself but the effort was beyond him. Dard watched grimly until it was over and then, fighting down a rising nausea, undertook the dirty business of retrieving his knife.

The sun did not show when he came out of the barn with Dessie after some hours which he did not want to remember. From a gray sky whirled flakes of white. Dard regarded them blankly at first and then with a dull relief.

A snow storm would hide a lot. Not that anyone would ever find Lars poor twisted body, now safely walled up in the passage. But Folley's people might be detained by a heavy storm if they started a search. The landsman had been a tyrant and the district bully—not beloved enough to arouse interest for a sizable searching party.

"Where are we going, Dardie?" Dessie's voice was a monotone. She had not cried, but she had shivered continually, and now she looked at the outer world with a shadow of dread in her eyes. He drew her closer as he shouldered their bag of supplies.

"Into the woods, Dessie. We'll have to live as the animals do—for a while. Are you hungry?"

She did not meet his eyes as she shook her head. And she made no effort to move until his hand on her shoulder drew her along. The snow thickened in a wild dance, driven by gusts of wind to hide the still smoldering cellar of the farmhouse. Pushing Dessie before him Dard began the hike back along his path of the night before—toward the hollow tree and the meeting place. To contact Lars' messenger might now be their only chance.

Under the trees the fury of the storm was less, but the snow packed against their bodies, clinging to their eyelashes and a wisp of hair which hung across Dessie's forehead so that she brushed at it mechanically. Food, heat, shelter, their needs made a pattern in Dard's mind and he clung to it, shutting out memories of the past night. Dessie could not stand this tramping for long. And he was almost to the end of his own strength. He used the rifle as a staff.

The rifle—and three shells—— He had those. But he dared not use the weapon except as a last resort. The sound of a shot carried too far. There were only a few guns left and they were in the hands of those whom the Peacemen had reason to trust. Anyone hunting for Folley would be attracted by a shot. If their escape became suspected. . . . He shivered with something other than cold.

Herding Dessie at a steady pace he fought his way to the hollow tree. There was no need to worry about the trail they had left, the snow filled it in a matter of minutes. But they must stay near here—for Lars' messenger to find them.

Dard set Dessie to treading back and forth in a space he marked out for her. That not only kept her moving and so fighting the insidious cold numbness, but it packed down a flooring for the shelter he built. A fallen tree gave it backing and pine branches, heaped up and covered with snow, provided a roof.

He could see the hollow in the tree from this lair and he impressed upon Dessie the necessity of watching for anyone coming along the path.

They ate handfuls of snow together with wooden bits of salted meat. But the little girl complained of sleepiness and at last Dard huddled in the shelter with Dessie in his arms, the rifle at hand, fighting drowsiness to keep his grim vigil.

At length he had to put the rifle between his feet, the end of the barrel just under his jaw, so that when he nodded, the touch of the cold metal nudged him into wakefulness. How long they dared stay there was a question which continued to trouble him. What if the messenger did not come today or tomorrow? There was a cave back in the hills which he had discovered during the past summer but—

The jab of the rifle barrel made his eyes water with pain. The snow had stopped falling. Branches, heavily burdened, were bent to the ground, but the air was free. He pulled back his top covering and studied Dessie's pinched face. She was sleeping, but now and again she twisted uneasily and once she whimpered. He changed position to aid his cramped legs and she half roused.

But right on her inquiring "Dardie?" came another sound and his hand clamped right across her lips. Someone was coming along the woods trail, singing tunelessly.

The messenger?

Before Dard's hope was fully aroused it was dashed. He saw a flash of red around a bush and then the wearer of

26

that bright cap came into full view. Dard's lips drew back in a half-snarl——

Lotta Folley!

Dessie struggled in his arms and he let her crawl to one side of the tiny shelter. But, though he brought up the rifle, he found he could not aim it. Hew Folley—betrayer and murderer—yes. His daughter—though she might be of the same brutal breed—though he might be throwing away freedom and life—he could not kill!

The girl, a sturdy stout figure in her warm homespuns and knitted cap, halted panting beneath the very tree he must watch. If she glanced up now—if her woodsight was as keen as his—and he had no reason to doubt that it was.

Lotta Folley's head raised and across the open expanse of snow her eyes found Dard's strained face. He made no move in a last desperate attempt to escape notice. After all he was in the half-shadow of the shelter, she might not see him—the protective "playing dead" of an animal.

But her eyes widened, her full mouth shaped a soundless expression of astonishment. With a kind of pain he waited for her to cry out.

Only she made no sound at all. After that first moment of surprise her face assumed its usual stupid, slightly sullen solidity. She brushed some snow from the front of her jacket without looking at it, and when she spoke in her hoarse common voice, she might have been addressing the tree at her side.

"The Peacemen are huntin'."

Dard made no answer. She pouted her lips and added, "They're huntin' you."

He still kept silent. She stopped brushing her jacket and her eyes wavered around the trees and brush walling in the old road.

"They say as how your brother's a stinkman——"

"Stinkman," the opprobious term for a scientist. Dard continued to hold his tongue. But her next question surprised him.

"Dessie—Dessie all right?"

27

He was too slow to catch the little girl who slipped by him to face the Folley girl gravely.

Lotta fumbled in the breast of her packet and brought out a packet folded in a piece of grease-blotted cloth. She did not move up to offer it to Dessie but set it down carefully on the end of a tree stump.

"For you," she said to the little girl. Then she turned to Dard. "You better not stick around. Pa tol' the Peacemen about you." She hesitated. "Pa didn't come back las' night—"

Dard sucked in his breath. That glance she had shot at him, had there been knowledge in it? But if she knew what lay in the barn—why wasn't she heading the hue and cry to their refuge? Lotta Folley, he had never regarded her with any pleasure. In the early days, when they had first come to the farm, she had often visited them, watching Kathia, Dessie, with a kind of lumpish interest. She had talked little and what she said suggested that she was hardly more than a moron. He had been contemptuous of her, though he had never showed it.

"Pa didn't come back las' night," she repeated, and now he was sure she knew—or suspected. What would she do? He couldn't use the rifle—he couldn't——

Then he realized that she must have seen that weapon, seen and recognized it. He could offer no reasonable explanation for having it with him. Folley's rifle was a treasure, it wouldn't be in the hands of another—and surely not in the hands of Folley's enemy—as long as Folley was alive.

Dard caught the past tense. So she did know! Now—what was she going to do?

"Pa hated lotsa things," her eyes clipped away from his to Dessie. "Pa liked t' hurt things."

The words were spoken without emotion, in her usual dull tone.

"He wanted t' hurt Dessie. He wanted t' send her t' a work camp. He said he was gonna. You better give me that there gun, Dard. If they find it with Pa they ain't gonna look around for anybody that ran away."

"But why?" he was shocked almost out of his suspicion.

"Nobody's gonna send Dessie t' no work camp," she stated flatly. "Dessie—she's special! Her ma was special, too. Once she made me a play baby. Pa—he found it an' burned it up. You—you can take care of Dessie—you gotta take care of Dessie!" Her eyes met his again compellingly. "You gotta git away from here an' take Dessie where none of them Peacemen are gonna find her. Give me Pa's rifle an' I'll cover up."

Driven to the last rags of his endurance Dard met that with the real truth.

"We can't leave here yet——"

She cut him off. "Some one comin' for you? Then Pa was right—your brother was a stinkman?"

Dard found himself nodding.

"All right," she shrugged. "I can let you know if they come again. But you see to Dessie—mind that!"

"I'll see to Dessie." He held out the rifle and she took it from him before she pointed again to the packet.

"Give her that. I'll try to git you some more—maybe tonight. If they think you got away they'll bring dogs out from town. If they do——" She shuffled her feet in the snow. Then she stood the rifle against the hollow tree and unbuttoned the front of her packet. Her hands, clumsy in mittens, unwound a heavy knitted scarf and tossed it to the child.

"You put that on you," she ordered with some of the authority of a mother, or at least of an elder sister. "I'd leave you my coat, only they'd notice." She picked up the rifle again. "Now I'll put this here where it belongs an' maybe they won't go on huntin'."

Speechless Dard watched her turn down trail, still at a loss to understand her actions. Was she really going to return that rifle to the barn—how could she, knowing the truth? And why?

He knelt to wind the scarf around Dessie's head and shoulders. For some reason Folley's daughter wanted to help them and he was beginning to realize that he needed all the aid he could get.

The packet Lotta had left contained such food as he had

not seen in years—real bread, thick buttered slices of it, and a great hunk of fat pork. Dessie would not eat unless he shared it with her, and he took enough to flavor his own meal of the wretched fare they had brought with them. When they had finished he asked one of the questions which had been in his mind ever since Lotta's amazing actions.

"Do you know Lotta well, Dessie?"

She ran her tongue around her greasy lips, collecting stray crumbs.

"Lotta came over often."

"But I haven't seen her since——" he stopped before mentioning Kathia's death.

"She comes and talks to me when I am in the fields. I think she is afraid of you and—Daddy. She always brings me nice things to eat. She said that some day she wanted to give me a dress—a pink dress. I would very much like a pink dress, Dardie. I like Lotta—she is always good—inside she is good."

Dessie smoothed down the ends of her new scarf.

"She is afraid of her Daddy. He is mean to her. Once he came when she was with me and he was very, very mad. He cut a stick with his knife and he hit her with it. She told me to run away quick and I did. He was a very bad man, Dardie. I was afraid of him, too. He won't come after us?"

"No!"

He persuaded Dessie to sleep again and when she awoke he knew that he must have rest himself and soon. Impressing upon her how much their lives depended on it, he told her to watch the tree and awaken him if anyone came.

It was sunset when he aroused from an uneasy, nightmare-haunted sleep. Dessie squatted quietly beside him, her small grave face turned to the trail. As he shifted his weight she glanced up.

"There was just a bunny," she pointed to small betraying tracks. "But no people, Dard. Is—is there any bread left? I'm hungry."

"Sure you are!" He crawled out of the shelter and

stretched cramped limbs before unwrapping the remains of Lotta's bounty.

In spite of her vaunted hunger Dessie ate slowly, as if savoring each crumb. The light was fading fast, although there were still red streaks in the sky. Tonight they must remain here—but tomorrow? If Lotta's return of the rifle to the barn did not stop the search—then tomorrow the fugitives would have to take to the trail again.

"Is it going to snow again, Dardie?"

He studied the sky. "I don't think so. I wish it would."

"Why? When the snow is deep, it's hard to walk."

He tried to explain. "Because when it snows, it is really warmer. Too cold at night . . ." he didn't finish that sentence, but encircled Dessie with a long arm and drew her back under the shelter with him. She wriggled about, settling herself more comfortably, then she jerked upright again.

"Someone's coming!" her whisper was warm on his cheek.

He had heard that too, the faint creak of a foot on the icy coated snow. And his hand closed about the haft of his knife.

3. THE CLEFT DWELLERS

HE WAS A SMALL MAN, the newcomer, and Dard overtopped him by four inches or more. And that gave the boy confidence enough to pull out of the shelter. He watched the stranger come confidently on, as though he knew just how many steps lay between himself and some goal. His clothing, what could be seen of it in the fast deepening dusk, was as ragged and patched as Dard's own. This was no landsman or Peaceman scout. Only one who did not hold all the important "confidence cards" would go about so unkempt. Which meant that he was an "unreliable," almost as much an outlaw as a techneer or a scientist.

The newcomer stopped abruptly in front of the tree. But he did not raise his hand to the hollow, instead he studied the tracks left by Lotta. But finally he shrugged and reached into the hole.

Dard moved and the other whirled in a half-crouch. There was the gleam of teeth in his bearded face, and another glint—of bare metal—in his hand.

But he made no sound and it was Dard who broke the quiet.

"I am Dard Nordis——"

"So? . . ." The single word was lengthened to approximate a reptile's hiss.

And Dard sensed that he was facing a dangerous man, a menace far worse than Hew Folley or any of his brutal kind.

"Suppose you tell me what has happened?" the man added.

"Roundup raid—last night," Dard returned laconically, his initial relief at the other's coming considerably dampened. "We thought we had escaped. I came up to leave that message for Lars." He motioned to the rag. "When I got back Lars was dead—killed by the neighbor who probably set them on us. So Dessie and I came here to wait for you."

"Peacemen!" the man spat. "And Lars Nordis dead! That's a bad piece of luck—bad." He made no move to put away the gun he held. It resembled a hand stun gun, but certain peculiarities of the stub barrel suggested that it was more deadly a weapon than that.

"And now," the man moved a step or two in Dard's direction, "what do you expect me to do with you?"

Dard moistened dry lips with a nervous tongue. He had not considered that, without Lars and what Lars had to offer, the mysterious underground might not wish to burden themselves with an untrained boy and a small child. Grim necessity was the law among all the present outlaws, and useless hands coupled with another mouth to feed were not wanted. He had a single hope. . . .

Lars had been so insistent about that word pattern that Dard dared now to believe that he must carry his brother's discovery in that memorized design of lines and numbers. He *had* to believe that and impress the importance of his information upon this messenger. It would be their passport to the underground.

"Lars had finished his work," Dard schooled his voice to conversational evenness. "I think you need the results——"

The man's head jerked. And now he did put away that oddly shaped gun.

"You have the formula?"

Dard took a chance and touched his own forehead. "I have it here. I'll deliver it when and if I reach the proper persons."

The messenger kicked moodily at a lump of snow. "It's a long trip—back into the hills. You have supplies?"

"Some. I'll talk when we're safe—when Dessie is safe——"

"I don't know—a child—the going's pretty tough."

"You'll find we can keep up," Dard made a promise he had no surety of keeping. "But we had better start now—there's just a chance that they may be after us."

The man shrugged. "All right. Come ahead—the two of you."

Dard handed the bag of supplies to the other and took Dessie's hand. Without another word the man turned to retrace the way he had come and the other two followed, keeping as well as they could to the trail he had broken.

They traveled on all that night. Dard first led and then carried Dessie, until, after one halt, the guide waved him on and raised the little girl to his shoulder, leaving Dard to stumble along unburdened. They rested at intervals but never long enough to relax, and Dard despaired of being able to keep up the pace. This messenger was a tireless machine, striding as might a robot along some hidden trail of which he alone knew the landmarks.

At dawn they were close to the top of a rise. Dard pulled himself up the last of a steep slope, panting, to discover the other waiting for him. With a jerk of his thumb, the man indicated the crest of the divide.

"Cave—camp——" he got out the two words stiffly and

put Dessie down. "Can you make it by yourself?" he asked her.

"Yes," her hand sought his confidently. "I'm a good climber."

There was a hint of smile, an awkward smile, pulling long forgotten muscles about his tight mouth. "You sure are, sister!"

The cave was fairly deep, the narrow entrance giving little hint of the wide room one found after squeezing through. It was a revelation to Dard as the guide snapped on a hand beam from a tiny carrying case he took from a ledge by the entrance. This was, the boy gathered, a regular camping place used by the underground travelers. He sank down on a bed of leaves and watched their companion pull out a black box, adjusting a dial on its side. Within seconds they began to feel the heat radiating from it. Free Scientist equipment all of this—all top contraband. Dard had dim pre-purge memories of such aids to comfort.

Dessie gave a sigh of pure content and curled up as close to that wonder as she could get. She watched with sleepy eyes the owner of this marvel break open a can of soup and pour its half-frozen contents into a pan which he set on top of the heating unit. He rummaged through the bag of supplies Dard brought, grunting at the scantiness of the pitiful collection.

"We didn't have much time to pack," said Dard, finally irritated by the other's unspoken contempt.

"What brought them down on you?" the man asked, squatting back on his heels. He had the strange gun out, checking the clip which carried its charge, squinting down its few inches of barrel.

"Who knows? There was a landsman—he wanted the farm. He was the one who shot Lars."

"Hmm——" The man peered into the now bubbling soup. "Then it may have been only a routine raid after all —sparked by just general malice?"

That, Dard gathered from his tone, was the answer more desired by this stranger. And his own thoughts went back to the last evening in the farm house when Lars had made his announcement of success. The raid had followed too aptly—almost as if Lars' discovery at all costs had to be prevented from reaching those who might make use of it. What *had* Lars been working on, and why was it so important? And did he, Dard Nordis, actually know anything about it?

"What's your name?" Dessie eyed their companion over the cup of soup he had poured for her. "I never saw you before——"

For the second time that shadow smile appeared on the guide's lips.

"No, you never saw me, Dessie. But I've seen you—several times. And you may call me Sach."

"Sach," she repeated. "That is a funny name. But this is very good soup, Sach. Is this a celebration?"

He looked startled. "Don't know about its being a celebration, Dessie. But it is going to be a day of sleep for all of us. We still have a long way to go. Suppose you bed down over there and close your eyes."

Dard was nodding over his own supply of food and a very short time later followed the same orders.

He awoke with a start. Sach was stooping over him, his grimed hand over Dard's mouth as he shook him by the shoulder. As soon as he saw the awareness in the boy's eyes, he dropped down on one knee to whisper:

"There's a 'copter circling—been up and around overhead for a half hour. Either we've been trailed or they've found out about this cave and put a watch on it. Now you listen and get this straight. What Lars Nordis was doing means more than life to the Cleft Dwellers. They've been waiting for the results of his last tests." He paused and in quite a different voice as if repeating some talisman added two words Dard had once heard from Lars, "Ad astra." Then in a harsh command he continued, "They've got to have it and have it quick. We're some five miles from the valley. Set a line straight to the peak you can see from this cave entrance and keep to it. Give me a good start and watch. If the 'copter follows me, then it's okay for you to make a break to reach the peak. Keep undercover all you can. There's only one long stretch where you cross the river that you have to be in the open."

"But you——" Dard was trying to pull his sleep scattered thoughts together.

"I'll go down slope the opposite way. If they are suspicious of this hiding hole and are watching it, they may take out after me. And I've played this type of hide and seek before, I know the game. You watch from the entrance while I go—now!"

Dard followed him to the narrow opening where Sach lingered just within the shadow listening. Now Dard could hear it too, the faint whine of a 'copter beating through the cold afternoon air. It grew to a steady drone, passed overhead, and faded. Sach still waited. Then he gave a curt nod to Dard and melted away.

The boy crawled to the very edge of the concealing overhang. Sach by some trick had won a good ten feet down slope. It would be difficult for anyone sighting him now to guess just where he had appeared from. He slid down, in only enough hurry to suggest that he was bolting from a position he considered dangerous.

Now the 'copter was on its way back—either on a routine sweep or because the dark figure of Sach had been sighted. He leaped into the shelter of a pine grown thicket, but not soon enough to escape detection. The 'copter circled down. There was a loud crack awaking echoes from the surrounding rocks. Somebody had shot at the fugitive.

"Dardie!"

"It's all right," the boy called reassuringly over his shoulder into the cave. "I'll be back in a minute."

Sach had probably wormed his way down to the edge of the deep woods. The 'copter made another smaller and tighter circle and came closer to the ground, to allow three men to leap into the snow. Before they could gain their feet and their balance a pencil of green light beamed a tight ray at one. He screamed and threshed the snow into a high shower of drift. The others threw themselves flat but continued to snake toward the wood from which that attack had come, and the 'copter swooped to spray death into the silent trees. Sach had not only drawn the attention of the trackers, he was using every means of keeping it on him. The 'copter soared above the trees, westward, away from the cave. When the two men broke into the brush undercover Dard watched them out of sight.

It would be evening soon. And the eastern slope was well provided with cover. There were sections of bare rock on the slope where no snow clung. Dard's eyes narrowed—footprints were easy to see from the air. But there was another way of getting down to the valley, one which would leave no such tell-tale traces. He went inside and clicked on the light Sach had left.

"Time to go, Dardie?" Dessie asked.

"First we eat." He made himself move deliberately. If Sach's information was right they still had a long trip before them. And they must not start it with empty stomachs. He used supplies recklessly before tying up enough of the remains to provide them with food for at least one more day.

"Where is Sach?" Dessie wanted to know.

"He had to go away. We will travel alone now. Eat all that, Dessie."

"I am," she answered almost peevishly. "I wish we could stay here. That box makes it so nice and warm."

For a moment Dard was tempted to do just that. To venture out on an unknown trail through the snow and cold when they could lay snug here seemed not only foolish but almost criminal, especially when it involved taking Dessie into the wilderness. But the urgency which had sent Sach out into the very mouth of danger to draw off pursuit could not be denied. If Sach believed that the information they carried was as important as that—— Well, they would uphold their part of the bargain. And there was always the fear in his mind since the coming of the 'copter, that the cave *had* been marked down and was known to the Peacemen.

It was dusk when they came out into the snap of the cruel night air. Dard pointed to the nearest ledge of bare rock sloping downward.

"We must walk along that ledge so as not to leave tracks in the snow."

Dessie nodded. "But where the rock ends, Dardie, what do we do then?"

"Wait and see!"

They edged along the ledge and it seemed to Dard that the chill struck up from the stone with double intensity. But Dessie flitted ahead and was teetering back and forth on the very edge as he caught up.

"Now," he told her, "we are going to jump. Into the big drift down there."

He had meant to make that leap first, and was tensing his muscles for the spring, when Dessie went over. Whether she had voluntarily thrown herself over or whether she had lost her balance he could not tell. But before he could move she had disappeared, and a plume of snow puffed to mark her landing place. Dard crouched there uncertainly until he saw the wave of an arm. Then he plunged, calculating his fall to land him apart from Dessie. He was a moment in the frosty air and then deep in snow which choked his mouth and blinded his eyes.

When they had fought their way out of the drift Dard glanced back up the slope. They had won into the shadow of the woods where their trail would be concealed from 'copter spies. His ruse had succeeded!

Now, he swung to the east, five miles Sach had said. Their progress would depend upon drifts and footing. It wouldn't be too hard going in the shelter of the trees. Luckily this was no dense forest. And by steering with the peak and the river they could reach their ultimate goal.

In the beginning the journey appeared simple and Dard was lighthearted. But before morning dawned they were caught in a nightmare. They had reached the river's bank, only to find the ice crust there too thin to use as a bridge. Time and time again, as they hunted along its bank, they sank knee deep into the powdery snow. Dard carried Dessie again and had to abandon the bag of supplies. He knew with a sinking heart that the periods of struggle between the rests were growing shorter and shorter. But he dared not give up and try to camp—being sure that if he once relaxed he would never rise again.

Morning found them at the one place where the river might be crossed. An arch of ice, snow crowned, made a perilous bridge over which they crept fearfully. The peak stood needle-pointing into the sky—probably, the boy thought bitterly, looking closer than it was.

He tried to keep to the cover afforded by brush and trees, but the rays of the rising sun reflected from the snow confused him and at last he plodded on, setting each foot down with exaggerated care, grimly determined only upon keeping his feet, with or without protection from a 'copter.

Dessie rested across his shoulder, her eyes half-closed. He believe that she was unconscious now, or very close to it. She gave no protest when he laid her body down on a fallen tree and leaned against another forest giant to draw panting gasps that cut his lungs with knives of ice. Some instinct or good fortune had kept him on the right course—the peak was still ahead. And now he could see that it guarded the entrance to a narrow cleft through which a small pathway led. But what lay beyond that cleft and how far he would still be from help if he could reach it he had no idea.

Dard allowed himself to rest until he had counted slowly to one hundred, and then he lifted Dessie again and lurched on, trying to avoid the clutching briars on neighboring bushes. In that moment, as he straightened up with the girl in his arms, he thought that he had sighted a strange glint of light from near the crown of the peak. Sun striking on ice, he reasoned dully as he plodded on.

He was never to know if he could have made the last lap of that journey under his own power. For, before he had gone a hundred yards, his fatigue-dulled ears caught the ominous sound of a 'copter engine. And, without trying to locate the source, he threw himself and his burden into the bushes, rolling through the snow and enduring the lash of branches.

The whine of the machine's supporting blades sounded doubly clear through the morning air. And a second later he saw splinters fly from a tree trunk not a foot away. Dragging Dessie he pulled back into thicker cover. But he knew that he was only prolonging the end. They knew that he was alone except for the child, they would conclude that he was unarmed. They had only to land men and take him at their leisure.

But, though the 'copter swept back and forth over the tangle of brush into which he had burrowed his way, it made no move to land anyone. So, thinking that he now was screened from their sight, Dard squatted down holding Dessie tightly, trying to think.

Sach—Sach and the green ray which had brought down the Peacemen back on the heights by the cave; that was it. They knew that he carried no rifle. But they were afraid that he might be armed with one of those more potent weapons such as Sach had used. Dessie whimpered and clung closer to him as the 'copter made another dive above their hiding place—one which leveled off only inches above the branches which might have tangled in the under-carriage.

The crack of rifle fire punctuated the whine of the engine. Again he watched splinters fly—one close enough to score his cheek. By will alone he held himself immovable and kept Dessie captive, though her little body flinched at the sound of each shot. Those above could not see their quarry or they would not be spraying bullets so indiscriminantly. This raking of the brush was to force him out.

And the worst of it was that they could do just that! Dard knew that the searching stream of death quartering the thicket would either kill them or force them to move.

He blinked at the bushes and made his first constructive move, stripping Lotta's scarf off Dessie's head and shoulders. Quickly he tangled the thick wool in some thorned branches. Then he put Dessie on her knees in the snow and pushed her away from that thorn bush. She obediently wormed her way off as Dark followed, moving by inches. Luckily the 'copter was now making the rounds of the perimeter of the thicket and for a minute or two there had been no shooting. Dard traveled on until the scarf end pulled taut in his hand, until he could keep his grip on the loose end only with thumb and forefinger at the full extent of an out-stretched arm. Then he lay waiting.

The 'copter was moving in again while more than one marksman added to a crisscross fire. Dard bit deep on the soft inner side of his lip. Now! By the sound the 'copter was just in the right position. As a rifle cracked, Dard gave two quick jerks of the scarf, and was answered by a loud burst of fire. Then he screamed wildly, and Dessie, shocked out of her bewilderment, echoed him thinly. Another tug at the scarf for good measure and then he was racing on hands and knees, bumping Dessie before him. If they would only believe that he, or Dessie, or both had been hit! That should bring them down, set them fighting their way to the spot where he had fastened the scarf. And then there would be a slim chance, a terribly slim chance, to get away.

Dard cringed at the sound of the vicious attack the 'copter riders were still centering behind him—an attack delivered without any call to surrender. All that blind hatred which had boiled over during the purge was still smoldering in those who were now hunting them. He had always known that anyone of proven scientist blood would have little chance if the Peacemen tracked him down, but now the last faint hope of mercy for the helpless was gone.

Pulling Dessie he reached the end of the thicket in which they had taken refuge. By some blind chance they had come out on the side which faced the peak. But before them lay a wide open sweep of ground, impossible to cross undetected. Dard faced it bleakly. The brightness of the sunlight somehow made that last blow harder.

But, even as his misery and despair weakened him, he suddenly noted again flashes of light on the peak—coming in too regular a pattern to be sun fostered. While he was still gaping up at that, a shadow swept over. The 'copter landed directly on that virgin expanse of snow before him. He sagged and his arms tightened about Dessie who gave a muffled cry as his grip hurt her. This was the end—they could not run any more.

The Peacemen were taking their time about leaving the 'copter. It looked as if they were still reluctant to approach that thicket. What had Sach done that made them so wary?

Two of them crept around the tail of the machine, and Dard saw the gun mounted on the 'copter's roof swing about to cover them. The men crawled slowly through the snow. But before they had reached beyond the length of the 'copter, that blink of light on the peak stepped up into a steady glow. Dard's eyes dropped from it to the Peacemen and so he did not see deliverance arrive.

There was a swish of sound followed by a tinkle as if glass had splintered. Green fog bellowed out about the machine—the same fatal green of the ray Sach had used on the cave slope.

Without knowing why, he threw himself face down, carrying Dessie with him, as traces of the fog wafted slowly toward the thicket. It must be gas, and those men were now floundering in it. Then the world went black and Dard fell into deep space, a place where Dessie, too, was swept away from him.

4. AD ASTRA

DARD LAY ON HIS back staring up into unfamiliar gray reaches. Then a pinkish globe swam into position over him and he concentrated upon it. Eyes, nose, a mouth that was opening and shutting, took proper place.

"How is it, fella?"

Dard considered the question. He had been face down in the snow, there had been Peacemen creeping after him and—Dessie! Dessie! He struggled to sit up and the face of that figure above him moved.

"The little girl, she's all right. You're both all right now. You *are* the Nordis kids?"

Dard nodded. "Where is here?" he formed the inquiry slowly. The face crinkled into laughter.

"Well, at least that's a variation on the old 'where am I?' You're in the Cleft, kid. We saw you trying to make it across the river valley with that 'copter after you. You managed to delay them long enough for us to lay down the fog. Then we gathered you in. Also we're a 'copter and some assorted supplies to the good, so you've more than paid your admittance fee—even if you weren't Lars Nordis' kin."

"How did you discover who we are?" Dard asked.

Dark brown eyes twinkled. "We have our little ways of learning what is necessary for us to know. And it is a painless process—done while you're asleep."

"I talked in my sleep? But I don't!"

"Maybe not under ordinary circumstances. But let our medico get the digester on you and you do. You've had a pretty hard pull, kid, haven't you?"

Dard levered himself up on his elbows and the other slipped extra support behind him. Now he could see that he was stretched out on a narrow cot in a room which seemed to be part cave, for three of its walls were bare rock, the fourth a smooth gray substance cut by a door. There were no windows, and a soft light issued from two tubes in the rock ceiling. His visitor perched on a folding stool and there was no other furniture in the cell-like chamber.

But there were coverings over him such as he had not seen for years, and he was wearing a clean, one piece coverall over a bathed body. He smoothed the top blanket lovingly. "Where is here—and what is here?" he expanded his first question.

"This is the Cleft, the last stronghold, as far as we know, of the Free Men." The other got to his feet and stretched. He was a tall, lean-waisted man, with dark brown skin, against which his strong teeth and the china-white of his eyeballs made startling contrast. Curly black hair was cropped very close to his round skull, and he had only a slight trace of beard. "This is the gateway to Ad Astra——" he paused, eyeing Dard as if to assess the effect those last two words had on the boy.

"Ad Astra," Dard repeated. "Lars spoke of that once."

"Ad Astra means 'to the stars.' And this is the jumping off place."

Dard frowned. To the stars! Not interplanetary—but galactic flight! But that was impossible!"

"I thought that Mars and Venus——" he began doubtfully.

"Who said anything about Mars or Venus, kid? Sure, they're impossible. It would take most of the resources of a willing Terra to plant a colony on either of them—as who should know better than I? No, not interplanetary flight—stellar. Go out to take our pick of waiting worlds such as earth creepers never dreamed of, that's what we're going to do! Ad Astra!"

Galactic flight—his first wild guess had been right.

"A star ship here!" In spite of himself Dard knew a small thrill far inside his starved body. Men had landed on Mars and Venus back in the days before the Burn and the Purge, discovering conditions on both planets which made them almost impossible for human life without a vast expenditure which Terra was not willing to make. And, of course, Pax had forbidden all space flight as part of the program for stamping out scientific experimentation. But a *star* ship—to break the bounds of Sol's system and go out to find another sun, other planets. It sounded like a very wild dream but he could not doubt the sincerity of the man who had just voiced it.

"But what did Lars have to do with this?" he wondered aloud. Lars' field had been chemistry, not astronomy or the mechanics of space flight. Dard doubted whether his brother could have told one constellation from another.

"He had a very important part. We've just been waiting around for you to wake up to get the report of his findings."

"But I thought you got the full story out of me while I was unconscious."

"What you personally did in the past few days, yes. But you do carry a message from Lars, don't you?" For the first time some of the dark man's lightheadedness vanished.

Dard smoothed the blanket and then plucked at it with nervous fingers. "I don't know—I hope so—"

His companion ran his hands across his tight cap of hair.

"Suppose we have Tas in. He's only been waiting for you to come around." He crossed the room and pushed a wall button.

"By the way," he said over his shoulder, "I'm forgetting introductions. I'm Simba Kimber, Pilot-astrogator Simba Kimber," he repeated that title as if it meant a great deal to him. "And Tas is First Scientist Tas Kordov, biological division. Our organization here is made up of survivors from half a dozen Free Scientist teams as well as quite a few just plain outlaws who are not Pax-minded. Oh, come in, Tas."

The man who entered was short and almost as broad as he was tall. But sturdy muscle, not fat, thickened his shoulders and pillared his arms and legs. He wore the faded uniform of a Free Scientist with the flaming sword of First Rank still to be picked out on the breast. His eyes and broad cheek bones had Tartar contour and Dard believed that he was not a native of the land in which he now lived.

"Well, and now you are awake, eh?" he smiled at Dard. "We have been waiting for you to open those eyes—and that mouth of yours—young man. What word do you bring from Lars Nordis?"

Dard could hesitate about telling the full truth no longer. "I don't know whether I have anything or not. The night the roundup gang came Lars said he had finished his job——"

"Good!" Tas Kordov actually clapped his hands.

"But when we had to clear out he didn't try to bring any papers with him——"

Kordov's face was avid as if he would drag what he wanted out of Dard by force. "But he gave to you some message—surely he gave some message!"

"Only one thing. And I don't know how important that may be. I'll have to have something to write on to explain properly."

"Is that all?" Kordov pulled a notebook out of his breeches' pocket and flipped it open to a blank page, handing it to him with an inkless stylus. Dard, equipped with the tools, began the explanation which neither of these men might believe.

"It goes way back. Lars knew that I imagine words as designs. That is, if I hear a poem, it makes a pattern for me—" he paused trying to guess from their expressions whether they understood. Somehow it didn't sound very sensible now.

Kordov pulled his lower lip away from his yellowish teeth and allowed it to snap back. "Hmm—semantics are not my field. But I believe that I can follow what you mean. Demonstrate!"

Feeling foolish, Dard recited Dessie's jingle, marking out the pattern on the page.

"Eesee, Osee, Icksie, Ann; Fullson, Follson, Orson, Cann."

He underlined, accented, and overlined, as he had that evening on the farm and Dessie's kicking legs came into being again.

"Lars saw me do this. He was quite excited about it. And then he gave me another two lines, which for me do not make the same pattern. But he insisted that this pattern be fitted over his lines."

"And those other lines?" demanded Tas.

Dard repeated the words aloud as he jotted them down.

"Seven, nine, four and ten; twenty, sixty and seven again."

Carefully he fitted the lines through and about the numbers and handed the result to Kordov. To him it made no possible sense, and if it didn't to the First Scientist, then he would not have had Lars' precious secret at all. When Tas continued to frown down at the page, Dard lost the small flicker of confidence he had had.

"Ingenious," muttered Kimber looking over the First Scientist's shoulder. "Could be a code."

"Yes," Tas was going to the door. "I must study it. And look upon the other notes again. I must——"

With that he was gone. Dard sighed.

"It probably doesn't mean a thing," he said wearily. "But what should it be?"

"The formula for the 'cold sleep,' " Kimber told him.

"Cold sleep?"

"We go to sleep, hibernate, during that trip—or else the ship comes to its port manned by dust! Even with all the improvements they have given her—the new drive—everything—our baby isn't going to make the big jump in one man's lifetime, or in a number of lifetimes!" Kimber paced back and forth as he talked, turning square corners at either end of the room. "In fact, we didn't have a chance—we'd begun thinking of trying to make a stand on Mars—before one of our men accidentally discovered Lars Nordis was alive. Before the purge he'd published one paper concerning his research on the circulatory system of bats—studying the drop in their body temperature during their winter sleep. Don't ask me about it, I'm only a pilot-astrogator, not a Big Brain! But he was on the track of something Kordov believed might be done—the freezing of a human being so that he can remain alive but in sleep indefinitely. And since we contacted him, Lars has continued to feed us data bit by bit."

"But why?" Why, if Lars had been working with this group so closely, hadn't he wanted to join them? Why had they had to live in a farmhouse on a starvation level, under constant fear of a roundup?

"Why didn't he come here?" It was as if Kimber had picked that out of Dard's mind. "He said he wasn't sure he could make the trip—crippled as he was. He didn't want to try it until the last possible moment when it wouldn't matter if he were sighted trying—or traced here. He believed that he was under constant surveillance by some enemy and that the minute he, or any of you, made a move out of the ordinary, that enemy would bring in the Peacemen, perhaps before he had the answer to our problem. So you had to live on a very narrow edge of safety."

"Very narrow," Dard agreed. There was logic in what Kimber said. If Folley had been spying on them, and he must have or else he would not have appeared in the barn, he would have suspected something if any of them had not shown around the house as usual. Lars could never have made the journey they had just taken. Yes, he could see why his brother had waited until it was too late for him.

"But there's something else." Kimber sat down on the stool again, his elbows resting on his knees, his chin supported by his cupped hands.

"What do you know about the Temple of the Voice?"

Dard, still intent upon the problem of the cold sleep, was startled. Why did Kimber want to know about the innermost heart of the neighboring Pax establishment?

The "Voice" was that giant computer to which representatives of Pax fed data—to have it digested and to receive back the logical directives which enabled them to control the thousands under their rule. He knew what the "Voice" was, had had it hazily described to him by hearsay. But he doubted whether any Free Scientist or any associate of such proscribed outlaws had ever dared to approach the "Temple" which housed it.

"It's the center of the Pax—" he began, only to have the pilot interrupt him.

"I mean—give me your own description of the place."

Dard froze. He hoped that his panic at that moment was not open enough to be marked. How did they know he had been to the Temple—through that mysterious digester which had picked over his memories while he was unconscious?

"You were there—two years ago," the other bored in relentlessly.

"Yes, I was there. Kathia was sick—there was just a chance of getting some medico to attend her if I could show a 'confidence card.' I made a Seventh Day visit but when I presented my attendance slip to the Circle they asked too many questions. I never got the card."

Kimber nodded. "It's okay, kid. I'm not accusing you of being a Pax plant. If you had been that, the digester would have warned us. But I have a very good reason for wanting to know about the Temple of the Voice. Now tell me everything you can remember—every detail."

Dard began. And discovered that his memory was a vivid one. He could recall the number of steps leading into the inner court and quote closely enough every word that the "Laurel Crowned" speaker of that particular Seventh Day had spouted in his talk to the faithful. When he finished he saw that Kimber was regarding him with an expression of mingled amazement and admiration.

"Good Lord, kid, how do you remember everything—just from one short visit?"

Dard laughed shakily. "What's worse, I can't forget anything. I can tell you every detail of every day I've lived since the purge. Before then," his hand went to his head, "before then for some reason it's not so clear."

"Lots of us would rather not remember what happened since then. You get a pack of fanatics in control—the way Renzi's forces have taken over this ant hill of a world—and things crack wide open. We've organized our collective sanity to save our own lives. And there's nothing we can do about the rest of mankind now—when we're only a handful of outlaws hiding out in the wilderness. There's a good big price on the head of everyone here in the Cleft. The whole company of Pax would like nothing better than to round us up. Only we're planning to get away. That's why we have to have the help of the Voice."

"The Voice?"

Kimber swept over the half interruption. "You know what the Voice is, don't you? A computer—mechanical brain they used to call them. Feed it data, it digests the figures and then spews out an answer to any problem which would require months or years for a human mind to solve. The astrogation course, the one which is going to take us to a sun enough like Sol to provide us with a proper world, is beyond the power of our setting up. We have the data and all our puny calculations—but the Voice has to melt them down for us!"

Dard stared at this madman. No one but a Peaceman who had reached the rarified status of "Laurel Wearer" dared approach the inner sanctuary which held the Voice. And just how Kimber proposed to get there and set the machine to work on outlawed formula, he could not possibly guess.

Kimber volunteered no more information and Dard did not ask. In fact he half forgot it during the next few hours as he was shown that strange honeycomb fortress, blasted out of the living rock, which served the last of the Free Scientists as a base. Kimber was his guide and escort along the narrow passages, giving him short glimpses of Hydro-gardens, of strange laboratories, and once, from a vantage point, the star ship itself.

"Not too large, is she?" the pilot had commented, eyeing the long silvery dart with a full-sized frown. "But she's the best we could do. Her core is an experimental model designed for a try at the outer planets just before the purge. In the first days of the disturbance they got her here—or the most important parts of her—and we have been building ever since."

No, the ship wasn't large. Dard frankly could not see where all the toiling inhabitants of the Cleft were going to find berths on her, whether in the suspended animation of hibernation or not. But he didn't mention that aloud. Instead he said:

"I don't see how you've been able to hide out without detection this long."

Kimber grinned wickedly. "We have more ways than one. What do you think of this?" He drew his hand from his breeches' pocket. On his dark palm lay a flat piece of shining metal.

"That, my boy, is gold! There's been precious little of it about for the past hundred years or so—governments buried their supplies of it and sat tight on them brooding. But it hasn't lost its magic. We have found many metals in these mountains and, while this is useless for our purposes, it still carries a lot of weight out there." He pointed to the peak which guarded the entrance to the Cleft. "We have our trading messengers and we fill hands in proper places. Then this is all camouflaged. If you were to fly across this valley in a 'copter, you'd see only what our techneers want you to. Don't ask me how they do it—some warping of the light rays—too deep for me." He shrugged. "I'm only a pilot waiting for a job."

"But if you are able to keep hidden, why 'Ad Astra'?"

Kimber rubbed the curve of his jaw with his thumb. "For several reasons. Pax has all the power pretty well in its hands now, so the Peacemen are stretching to wipe out the last holes of resistance. We've been receiving a steady stream of warnings through our messengers and the outside men we've bought. The roundup gangs are consolidating—planning on a big raid. What we have here is the precarious safety of a rabbit crouching at the bottom of a burrow while the hound sniffs outside. We have no time for anything except the ship, preparing to take advantage of the thin promise for another future that it offers us. Lui Skort—he's a medico with a taste for history—gives Pax another fifty to a hundred years of life. And the Cleft can't last that long. So we'll try the chance in a million of going out—and it is a chance in a million. We may not find another earth-type planet, we may not ever survive the voyage. And, well, you can fill in a few of the other ifs, ands, and buts for yourself."

Dard still watched the star ship. Yes, a thousand chances of failure against one or two of success. But what an adventure! And to be free—out of this dark morass which stunted minds and fed man's fears to the point of madness— to be free among the stars!

He heard Kimber laugh softly. "You're caught by it, too, aren't you, kid? Well, keep your fingers crossed. If your brother's stuff works, if the Voice gives us the right course, if the new fuel Tang concocted will really take her through—why—we're off!"

Kimber seemed so confident that Dard dared now to ask that other question.

"She isn't very big. How are you going to stow away all the people?"

For the first time the space pilot did not meet his eyes.

With the toe of his shabby boot Kimber kicked at an inoffensive table savagely.

"We can stow away more than you would believe just looking at her, if we are able to use the hibernation process."

"But not all," Dard persisted, driven by some inner need to know.

"But not all," Kimber agreed with manifest reluctance.

Dard blinked, but now there was a veil between his eyes and the sleek, silver swell of the star ship. He was not going to question farther. There was no need to, and he had no desire for a straight answer. Instead he changed the subject abruptly.

"When are you going to try to reach the Voice?"

"As soon as I hear from Tas—"

"And what do you wish to hear from Tas?" came a voice from behind Dard. "That he has succeeded in making sense of gibberish and 'kicking legs' and all the rest of the fantastic puzzle this young man has dumped into his head? Because if that is what you wait for, wait no longer, Sim! The sense has been made and thanks to Lars Nordis and our messengers," Kordov's big paw of a hand reached up to give Dard's shoulder a reassuring squeeze, "we can now take off into the heavens at our will. We wait only for your part of the operation."

"Good enough." Kimber started to turn when Dard caught his arm.

"Look here. You've never been to the Temple of the Voice."

"Of course not," Tas cut in. "Is he completely crazy? Does one thrust one's hand into raw atomic radiation?"

"But I have! Maybe I can't work your computations but I can guide you in and out. And I know enough about the official forms to—"

Kimber opened his mouth, plainly to refuse, but again the First Scientist was too quick for him.

"Now that makes very good sense, Sim. If young Nordis has already been there—why, that is more than any of the rest of us have done. And in the disguise you have planned the risk is less."

The pilot frowned and Dard prepared for an outright refusal. But at last Kimber gave a half-nod. Tas pushed Dard after him.

"Go along with you. And mind you bring him back in one piece. We can do many things among us, but he remains our only space pilot, our only experienced astrogator."

Dard followed Kimber along rock passages, back through the maze of the Cleft dwelling to a flight of stairs crudely hacked from the stone. The stairs ended in a large room holding a 'copter which bore all the markings of a Pax machine.

"Recognize it? This is the one which you played tag with out in the valley. Now—get into this and hurry!"

From the 'copter he took a bundle of clothing which he pitched over to Dard. The boy put on the Peaceman's black and white, buckling around him as a finishing touch a belt supporting a hand stun gun. Although the clothes were large the fit was good enough to pass in the half-light of evening. And they had to visit the Voice at night to have any chance at all.

He took his place gingerly beside the pilot inside the 'copter. Overhead a cover had rolled back so that the sky was open to them. As Dard secretly gripped the edge of his seat Kimber took the controls. And Dard continued to hold on as the machine started the slow spiral up into the air.

5. NIGHT AND THE VOICE

DARD SURVEYED the country over which the 'copter flew. It required only a few minutes to cover the same rugged miles across which he and Dessie had fought their way. And he was sure that he saw traces of that trip left on the snow below.

The machine skimmed over the heights which concealed the cave. And then, for the first time in crowded hours, Dard remembered Sach. It was down this very slope that the messenger had led the chase.

"You've heard from Sach?" He was anxious to be reassured concerning that small, wary man.

But Kimber didn't reply at once. And when he did, Dard was aware of the reservations in his tone.

"No news yet. He hasn't reported at any of our contacts. Which reminds me—"

Under the pilot's control the 'copter swung to the right and headed away from the path Dard had followed into the hills. He was unreasonably glad that they were not going to wing over the charred ruins of the farmhouse.

Instead, within a short space, they were circling another farm, one in much better condition than the farm which had sheltered the Nordis family. In fact, the buildings gave such an air of Pax-blessed landsman prosperity that Dard wondered at Kimber's visiting the place. Only a man with the brightest of prospects under the new rule would dare to keep his buildings in such good repair. And the volume of smoke curling fatly from the chimney spoke of unlimited warmth and food, better conditions than anyone but a staunch supporter of the Company of Pax could attain.

Yet Kimber set the 'copter down without hesitation on a stretch of packed snow not too far from the house. Once down however the pilot made no move to leave the machine.

The house door opened and a man wearing the good farm homespun of an "approved" landsman—another Folley by all outward signs—crossed the yard. For one wild moment Dard was inclined to doubt the man beside him, being still more uneasy when the round plump face of the landsman was thrust close to the window of the 'copter.

Pale blue eyes in a weather-beaten face flicked over them both, and Dard did not miss the fact that they widened a fraction as they passed from Kimber's impassive face to his flashy uniform. The landsman turned and spat at a hound that approached, showing white teeth and growling.

"Time?" he asked.

"Time," Kimber returned. "Get moving on tonight if you can, Harmon."

"Sure we've been packin' some stuff already. Th' boy's got th' road cleared—"

Then those blue eyes slid back to Dard. "Who's th' youngster?"

"Nordis' brother. He got in with the Nordis girl. Lars is dead—raid."

"Yeah. Heard a rumor they all were—that th' roundup got 'em. Glad to know that ain't th' truth. Well—be seein' you—"

With a wave of the hand he headed back to the house. And Kimber took them aloft.

"I didn't think—" Dard began. Kimber chuckled.

"You didn't think a man such as Harmon would be one of us? We have some mighty odd contacts here and there. We have men who drove ground trucks and men who were first rank scientists—before the purge. There's Santee—he was a non-com of the old army—he can read and write his name—and he's an expert with weapons—to us he's as important a part of the Cleft as Tas Kordov, who is one of the world's greatest biologists. We ask only one thing of a man—that he believes in true freedom. And Harmon is going to be more important in the future. We may know how to grow hydro-style—you had a meal or two with us and know that—but an honest dirt farmer will be able to teach us all better tricks. Added to that, Harmon's been our biggest ace in the hole all along. He and his wife, their son, and their twin girls—they've been playing a mighty hard role for more than five years—doing it splendidly, too. But I can well believe that he welcomed my news that it is over. Double lives are tough going. Now, back to work."

The 'copter wheeled and flew due west into a sky now painted with sunset colors. It was warm inside the cabin, and the clothing about his thin body was the finest he had worn in years. Dard relaxed against the padded cushion, but far inside him was a warming spark of excitement, an excitement no longer completely darkened by fear—Kimber's confidence in himself, in the eventual success of their mission was comforting.

Below ran a ribbon of road, and by the churned snow, it was a well-traveled one. Dard tried to identify landmarks. But, never having seen the country from above, he could only guess that they were now being guided to town by that same artery which had tied Folley's holding and the tumbledown Nordis place to the overgrown village which was the nearest approach to a pre-Burn city.

Another farm road, rutted and used, cut into the main road and its curve was familiar. It was Folley's! And it had seen considerable travel since the storm. He thought briefly of Lotta—wondered if she had gone back to the message tree with some food for Dessie as she had promised. Dessie!

Dessie!

Hoping he could keep from revealing to Kimber his own secret problem, the one which had gnawed at him ever since he had seen the star ship, he asked a question:

"I didn't see any children in the Cleft."

Kimber was intent upon flying; when he answered it was with a faint touch of absent-mindedness.

"There're only two. Carlee Skort's daughter is three and the Winson boy—he's almost four. The Harmon twins are—ten, I think—but they don't live in the Cleft."

"Dessie is six—almost seven."

Kimber grinned. "Bright little trick, too, isn't she? Took to Carlee right away—after we had persuaded her you were going to recover. Last I heard she'd taken command in the nursery quarters. Carlee was surprised at how sensible she was."

"Dessie's a pretty big person," Dard said slowly. "She's old for her years. And she has a gift, too. She makes friends with animals—not just tame ones—but the wild things. I've seen them come right up to her. She insists that they talk."

Had he said too much? Had he labeled Dessie as one

so far outside the pattern that she would not "fit" into a ship's company where a farmer was considered important? But surely, a child's future was worth more than an adult's! Dessie must be considered—she must be!

"Carlee thinks she is quite a person, too." That was certainly noncommittal enough. But, although he did not know Carlee, her approbation was comforting to Dard. A woman, a woman with a little girl of her own, would see that another little girl would get a fair break. As for himself—resolutely he refused to think ahead for himself. Instead he began to watch the twilight-cloaked road and think of the problem immediately before them.

"The 'copter park is at the back of the Temple. And you can't fly over the building—nothing crosses the sacred roof."

"Then we circle. No use taking chances. Park well guarded?"

"I don't know. Only Peacemen get inside. But I'd think that in the dark, and with this machine—"

"We could brazen it out? Let us hope they don't ask for any recognition signals. I'm going to try to land as close to the edge as I can and in the darkest part—unless they have floodlights—"

"Town lights!" Dard interrupted, intent on the sparks of yellow. "The Temple is on that rise to the south. See!"

It was easy enough to see. The lights of the town houses were small and sickly yellow. But above and beyond them were concentrated bars of vivid blue and startling white, somehow garish and out of place against the purple-blue of the sky. Kimber circled.

The Temple occupied about a third of the rise which had been leveled off to form a wide platform. Behind the building itself was a floodlit space in which they could see a row of 'copters.

"Ten down there," Kimber counted, the lighting of the instrument panel showing the planes and hollows of his face. "You'd think they would have more. This is a center for their control and they don't do much raiding by night. Or at least they haven't in the past."

"They may now. They struck our place at night."

"Anyway, the fewer the better. Look, that's a nice long shadow—one of their floods must have burnt out. I'm going to see if I can bring us down in it!"

They lost speed, it was something like coasting, much like floating, Dard decided. Then the lights arose about them and a second later the undercarriage made contact. They didn't bounce. Kimber shook hands with himself vigorously, in congratulation.

"Now listen, kid," the pilot's voice was a faint murmur. "That's a stun gun you have in your belt. Ever use one?"

"No."

"It doesn't require training to point it and push the button. But you're not to do that unless I give the word, understand? You have only two charges and I have the same in mine—we can't afford to waste them. Nothing—absolutely nothing must happen to prevent our interview with the Voice!" There was a passionate determination in that. It was an order, delivered not only to Dard, but to Destiny or Fortune herself. "Afterward we may have to fight our way out—though I hope not. Then the stun guns will be our hope. But we've got to use bluff to get us in!"

The Peacemen hoarded the remains of pre-purge invention, Dard noted as he matched his steps to Kimber's across the park at an unhurried pace, but their maintenance of such appliances was not promising. Several of the floodlights were out and there were cracks in the concrete under his boots. There couldn't be too many techneers left in the slave-labor camps of the Temple gangs. Some day no 'copter would rise from this park, no light would burn. Had the leaders of Pax thought of that, or didn't they care? The old cities built by the techneers were rubble fit only for bats and birds. Now there were only grubby villages slipping back and back, with the wilderness edging down across the field to nibble at man's building.

So far they had not met anyone, but now they approached the western gate of the Temple and there was a guard. Dard straightened his shoulders, lifted his chin, summoned that arrogance of bearing which cloaked a Peaceman as tightly as the gaudy uniform. Kimber had the right presence. He strode along with a damn-devil air suitable to a Laurel Wearer. Dard did his best to copy that. But the boy couldn't quite suppress a half-sigh of relief when the guard did not attempt to stop them and they crossed the threshold unchallenged.

Of course, they were still far from the sanctuary of the Voice. And Dard's knowledge of the place would not take them farther than the second court.

Kimber stopped and touched his companion's sleeve. Together they slipped out of the direct path of the light up to the shadowed obscurity behind one of the massive pillars.

Before them lay the inner court where the commoners might gather—in fact were expected to gather—to hear words of wisdom as mouthed from the August Sayings of Renzi by one of the Laurel Wearers. It was now deserted. After dark none of those not "Wedded to the Inner Peace" dared enter the Temple. Which would make the venture more precarious since they would be alone among the Peacemen and might betray themselves by ignorance of custom. Dard's hand twitched, but he kept it off the stun gun.

"The Voice?"

Dard pointed to the archway at the other end of the inner court. What they sought lay beyond that, but where —he wasn't sure. Kimber went on, flitting from pillar to pillar, and Dard followed on a woodman's sure, silent feet. Twice they stiffened into inanimateness as others tramped into the open. Peacemen, two Laurel Wearers and, just as they had almost reached the archway, a third party—two shuffling labor slaves carrying a box under the malicious eye of a single lounging guard.

Kimber leaned back behind a pillar and drew Dard in beside him.

"Lots of traffic." The whispered comment was tinged with laughter and Dard saw that the pilot was smiling, an eager fire in his eyes.

They waited until slaves and guard were gone and then

stepped boldly into the open and through the archway. They were now in a wide corridor, not too well lighted, broken at regular intervals with open doorways through which came solid blocks of illumination to trap the passer-by. But Kimber went on with the assurance of one who had a perfect right to be where he was. He did not attempt to steal a look at any of the rooms—it was as if he had seen their contents a thousand times.

Dard marveled at his complete confidence. The Voice—where was it housed in this maze? He never suspected all this to lie beyond the inner court. They had neared the end of the corridor before Kimber slackened pace and began glancing from right to left. With infinite caution he tried the latch of a closed door. It gave, swinging silently open to disclose a flight of stairs leading down. Kimber's grin was wide.

"Down here! It has to be down—" his lips shaped the words.

Together they crept close to the edge of the stairway and peered over into a cavern where the best lighting arrangements of the Temple made little headway against a general gloom. The hollow went deep, it was the heart of the eminence upon which the Temple stood. And on the floor far below was the Voice—a bank of metal, faceless, tongueless, but potent.

Two guards stood at the bottom of the stairs, but their attitudes suggested that they had no fear of being called upon to carry out any duties. And on a curved bench before a board of dials and levers lounged a third man wearing the crimson and gold tunic of a second circle Laurel Wearer.

"The night shift," mouthed Kimber at Dard's ear, and then he sat down on the platform and proceeded to remove his boots. After a moment of hesitation Dard followed the pilot's example.

Kimber, boots swinging in one hand, started noiselessly down the staircase, hugging the wall. But he did not draw the gun at his belt and Dard obediently kept his own weapon sheathed.

It was not entirely quiet in the chamber. A drowsy hum from the internals of the Voice was echoed and magnified by the height and width of the place.

Kimber took a long time—or what seemed to Dard a very long time—to descend. When they were still on the last flight of steps above the guard the pilot reached out a long arm and pulled Dard tight against him, his lips to the boy's ear.

"I'll risk using my gun on that fellow on the bench. Then we jump the other two with these—"

He gestured with the boots. Four steps—five—side by side they crept down. Kimber drew his stun gun and fired. The noiseless charge of the ray hit its mark. The man on the bench twisted, turning a horribly contorted face to them before he fell to the floor.

In that same instant Kimber hurled himself out and down. There was one startled shout as Dard went out into space too. Then the boy struck another body and they went to the floor together in a kicking clawing fury. Dodging a blow Dard brought his boots down club fashion in the other's face. He struck heavily three times before hands clutched his shoulders and wrenched him off the now limp man. Kimber, a raw and bleeding scrape over one eye, shook him out of the battle madness.

Dard's eyes focused on the pilot as the terrible anger drained out of him. They tied the limp bodies with the men's own belts and lacings before Kimber took his place on the bench before the Voice.

He pulled a much-creased sheaf of papers from the breast of his blouse and spread them out on the sloping board beneath the first rank of push buttons. Dard fidgeted, thinking the pilot was taking entirely too long over that business.

But the boy had sense enough to keep quiet as Kimber rubbed his hands slowly together as if to clear them of moisture before raising his eyes to study the row upon row of buttons, each marked with a different symbol. Slowly, with a finicky touch and care, the pilot pressed one, another, a third. There was a change in the hum of the Voice, a faster rhythm, the great machine was coming to life.

Kimber picked up speed, stopping only now and again to consult his scrawled notes. His fingers were racing now. The hum deepened to a throb which, Dard feared, must certainly be noticeable in the Temple overhead.

The boy withdrew to the stairway, his attention as much on the door at the top as on Kimber. He drew his gun. As Kimber had said, the mechanism of the arm was childishly simple—one pointed it, pushed the button on the grip—easy. And he had two charges to use. Caressing the metal he looked back at the Voice.

Under the light Kimber's face displayed damp drops, and now and again he rubbed his hand across his eyes. He was waiting—his part of the job finished—waiting for the Voice to assimilate the data fed it and move in its ponderous way to solve the problem. But every minute they were forced to linger added to the danger of their position.

One of the captives rolled over on his side, and, over the gag they had forced into his jaws, his eyes blared red hate at Dard. The hum of the Voice faded to a lulling murmur. There was no other sound in the cavern. Dard crossed to touch Kimber's shoulder.

"How long?" he began.

Kimber shrugged without taking his eyes from the screen above the keyboard. That square of light remained obstinately empty. Dard could not stand still. He had no timekeeper, and he believed that they had been there too long —it might be close to morning. What if another shift of watcher and guards was due to come on presently?

A sharp demanding chime interrupted his thoughts. The screen was no longer blank. Across it slowly crawled formula, figures, equations. And Kimber scrambled to write them down in frantic haste, checking and rechecking each he scribbled. As the last set of figures faded from the screen the pilot hesitated and then pushed a single button far to the right on the board. A moment of waiting and five figures flashed into being on the screen.

Kimber read them with a sigh. He thrust the sheets of calculations back into safety, before, with a grin playing about his generous mouth, he leaned forward and pushed as many buttons as he could reach at random. Without pausing for the reply, though the Voice had gone into labor again, he joined Dard.

"That will give them something to puzzle out if they try to discover what we were after," he explained. "No reading that back. Not that I believe any of these poor brains would have the imagination to guess what brought us here. Now—speed's the thing! Up with you, kid."

Kimber took the steps at a gait Dard had a hard time matching. It was not until they stood directly before the corridor door that the pilot stopped to listen.

"Let us hope that they've all gone to bed and are good sound sleepers," he whispered. "We've had a lot of luck tonight and this is no time for it to run out."

The corridor was as empty as it had been on their first trip. Some of the blocks of light from the rooms were gone. They had only three such danger spots to cross now. Two they negotiated without trouble, but as they stepped into the third, it was broken by a moving shadow, a man was coming out of the room. He wore a scarlet and gold tunic, with more gold on it than Dard had ever seen before—plainly one of the hierarchy. And he stared straight at them with annoyance and the faint stirrings of suspicion.

"Pax!" the word was hardly the conventional and courteous greeting, it carried too much authority. "What do you here, brothers? These are the night watches—"

Kimber drew back into the shadows and the man unconsciously followed him, coming out into the corridor.

"What—" he began again when the pilot moved. Both his dark hands closed about the other's throat, cutting off voice and breath.

Dard caught the hands clawing at Kimber's hold and together they dragged the struggling captive through the archway into the dimly lighted inner court.

"Either you come quietly," Kimber hissed, "or you don't come at all. Make your choice quick."

The struggles ceased as Kimber pulled him on.

"Why try to take him?" Dard wanted to know.

Kimber's grin was no longer pleasant, it was closer to a wolfish snarl. "Insurance," he returned concisely. "We aren't out of this place yet. Now move!" He gave the captive a vicious shove, keeping one hand clamped on the nape of the other's neck, as the three moved on toward the outer door and freedom.

6. FIVE DAYS—FORTY-FIVE MINUTES

A GRILLE of bars and metal wire was down across the entrance of the outer court. When they reached it their captive snickered. He had snapped out of his first panic-surprise, and though he was quite helpless in Kimber's hands, the voice with which he asked a question now was entirely self-possessed.

"How do you propose to get past this?"

The pilot met that demand almost jauntily. "I suppose that this is equipped with a time lock?"

The Laurel Wearer did not reply to that, he had a second demand: "Who are you?"

"What if I should say—a rebel?"

But that was the wrong answer. The man's lips thinned to a single cruel line.

"So—" his half-whisper was soft but it promised deadly reprisals, "Lossler dares this, does he? Lossler!"

But Kimber had no time for that. He shoved the captive into Dard's ready hands before he applied a black disc to the grille's lock. There was a crackle, a shower of spitting sparks. Then Kimber struck the barrier with his shoulder and it yielded. Taking the prisoner with them, they went out into the freedom of the night.

The town was in darkness, a dark broken only by a

scattering of street lights. The full moon picked out light and shadow in vivid black and white across the snow on roofs and yards.

"March!" Kimber pushed the captive before him in the direction of the 'copter park. Dard trotted behind, nervously alert, not yet daring to believe that they had been successful.

Before they came onto the crumbling concrete of the take-off Kimber had instructions for the Laurel Wearer.

"We're going to take a 'copter," he explained—bored—as if he were discussing a dull report, "and, once we do that, we shall have no more use for you, understand? It remains entirely up to you in what condition you shall be left behind—"

"And you can tell Lossler from me," the words came slowly, ground out one by one between teeth set close together, "that he is not going to get away with this!"

"Only we are getting away with it, aren't we? Now step right ahead—we are all friends—in case there is a guard on duty. You shall see us off and we will trouble you no more."

"But why?" protested the other. "What did you want here?"

"What did we want? That is a minor problem and you shall have all the rest of the night to solve it—if you can. Now, where's the guard?"

When the man made no answer Kimber's hand moved and brought a gasp of pain from the captive.

"Where—is—the—guard?" repeated the pilot, his patience iced by frigid promise of worse things to come.

"Three guards—gate and patrol—" came the gritted return.

"Excellent. Try to answer more promptly next time. You shall escort us through the gate. We are being sent by you on a special mission."

Just as Dard saw the black and white coat at the entance the command snapped out:

"Halt!"

Kimber obediently brought their procession of three to a stop.

"Speak your piece," he whispered.

"Pax, brother."

Dard was alert—waiting for some warning to that sentry. But Kimber must have taken precautions, for the voice of the Laurel Wearer sounded natural.

"Laurel Wearer Dawson on special business on the Company—"

The guard saluted. "Pass, Noble Dawson!"

Dard closed in on the heels of Kimber and Dawson with all the military bearing he could muster. He held the pose until they were passing along the row of idle 'copters. Then Kimber spoke to his fellow conspirator.

"There's the little matter of fuel. Climb into that baby and check the reading on the top dial in the row directly before the control stick. If it registers between forty and sixty—sing out. If it doesn't, we'll have to try the next."

Dard crawled into the seat and found the light button. Between—between forty and sixty! White figures danced crazily until he forced his nerves under control. "Fifty-three," he called out softly.

What Kimber intended to do with Dawson Dard never learned. For, at the moment, the Laurel Wearer gave a sudden heave, throwing himself down and trying to drag the pilot with him. At the same time he shouted, and that cry must have carried not only across the field, but into the Temple as well.

Dard hurled himself at the door of the 'copter. But before he could get out he saw an arm rise and fall in a deadly blow. A second scream for help was cut off in the middle and the pilot jumped for the machine. Dard found himself face down while the pilot scrambled over him to the controls. The 'copter lurched, the open door banging until Kimber was able to pull it to. They were air borne, and not a moment too soon as the whip crack of a shot testified.

The boy pulled up on the seat, trying to see behind them. Was that another 'copter rising? Or would they have more of a start before pursuit would be on their tail?

"Couldn't expect our luck to last forever," Kimber mur-

mured. "How about it, kid? Do they have anything up yet? Evasive action right now would be tough."

There was an ominous wink of red light now in the sky.

"Someone's coming up—wing lights showing."

"Wing lights, eh? Well, well, well, aren't we both the forgetful boys though." Kimber's hand went out to snap down a small lever.

From the corner of his eye Dard saw their own tell-tale wing-tip gleams disappear. But the pursuer made no move to shut his off—or else he did not care if he betrayed his position.

"I have now only one question," the pilot continued, half to himself. "Who is Lossler and why did our dear friend back there expect trouble from him? A split within the ranks of Pax—it smells like that. Too bad we didn't know about this Lossler complication sooner."

"Would such a split make any difference in your plans?"

"No, but we could have had a lot more fun these past few months. And playing one group against the other might have paid off. Like tonight—this Lossler may take the blame for us, and no one will come nosing around the Cleft for the crucial time we have left here. What the—!"

Kimber's body strained forward, he was suddenly intent upon the dials before him. Then he reached out to rap smartly on the very indicator he had told Dard to check before they had taken the 'copter. The needle behind the cracked glass remained as stationary as if it were painted across the numbers it half obscured. A line drew Kimber's brows together. Again he struck the glass, trying to jar loose the needle. Then he settled back in the seat.

"Dear me," he might have been remarking on the brightness of the night, "now we do have a problem. How much fuel? Is the tank full, part full, or deuced near empty? I thought this was all a little too smooth. Now we may have to—"

The smooth purr of the motor caught in a cough, and then picked up beat again. But Kimber shrugged resignedly.

"It is now not a question of 'may have to,' that cough was a promise that we *are* going to walk. How about our friend behind?"

"Coming strong," Dard was forced to admit.

"Which makes the situation very jolly indeed. We could do with less of this blasted moonlight! A few clouds hanging about would help."

The engine chose that moment to cough again and this time the pickup was delayed longer than before.

"Three or four drops more, maybe. Better set her down before we have to pancake. Now where're a lot of nice dark shadows? Ha—trees! And there's only one 'copter behind us—sure?"

"Sure." Dard verified that point before he answered.

"So, we have to do it the hard way. Here we go, m'lad."

The 'copter came down a field away from the road they had followed, landing heavily in a sizable drift. On the other side of a low wall was a clump of trees. And—Dard was pretty sure—he had sighted the outline of a house beyond.

They scrambled out and jumped the wall, struggling out of the soft snow into the grove. From behind came the sound of the other 'copter. Those in it must have sighted the machine on the ground at once, they were heading unerringly toward it.

"There's a house that way," Dard panted as Kimber plowed ahead with the determination of breaking beyond the thin screen of trees.

"Any chance of finding some transportation there?"

"None of the landsmen have surface cars any more. Folley had a double A rating, and Lotta said his application for one was turned down twice. Horses—maybe . . ."

Kimber expelled a snort. "Horses, yet!" he addressed the night. "And me not knowing which end of the animal is which!"

"We'd get away faster mounted," Dard sputtered as he slipped on a piece of iced crust and fell into the spiky embrace of a bush. "They'll probably put hounds on us—we're so near to town.

Kimber's pace slowed. "I'd forgotten those pleasures of civilization," he observed. "Do they use dogs a lot in tracking?"

"Depends on how important the tracked are."

"And we're probably number one on their list of public enemies now. Yes, nothing like being worthy of dogs—and no meat to throw behind us! All right, let's descend upon this house and see how many horses or reasonable facsimile of same we can find."

But when they reached the end of the grove they stopped. Lights showed in three house windows and they reached far enough across the snow-crusted road to reveal a 'copter there. Kimber laughed without any amusement at all.

"That bird by the machine is waving a rifle."

"Wait!" Dard caught at the pilot as Kimber started out of the brush.

Yes, he had been right—there was another 'copter coming! He felt Kimber tense in his hold.

"If they have any brains at all," the pilot whispered, "they'll box us up! We've got to get out."

But Dard held him fast.

"You're trying for the road," the boy objected.

"Of course! We daren't get lost now—and that is our only guide back. Or do you know this country well enough to go skating off into the midst of nowhere?"

Dard kept his hold on the other. "I know something—that this is the only road leading to the mountains, yes. But we can't take it unless . . ."

He took his hands from Kimber and pulled up the edge of the jacket he wore—the black jacket trimmed in white. With numb fingers he pulled buttons roughly out of holes and stripped off the too large garment. He had been right! The black fabric was completely lined with the same white which made the deep cuffs and the throat-fretting stand-up collar. And the breeches were white, too. With frantic haste he thrust sleeves wrongside out. Kimber watched him until he caught on and a minute later the pilot was reversing his own coat. White against white—if they kept in the ditches—if dogs were not brought—they still had a thin chance of escaping notice.

They half fell, half plunged into the ditch beside the road just as a second 'copter came to earth. Dard counted at least six men fanning out in a circle from it, beginning a stealthy prowl into the grove they had left.

Neither of the futitives waited longer, but, half crouched, scurried along between the dry brush which partly filled the ditch and the ragged hedges walling the fields. The skin between Dard's shoulder blades crawled as he expected momentarily to feel the deadly impact of a bullet. Tonight death was a closer companion than the pilot whose boots kicked snow into his sweating face.

Some time later they reached the curve of a farm lane and dared to venture out in the open to skim across it. The cold pinched at them now. As warm as the uniform had seemed when they rode in the heated 'copter cabin, it was little defense against the chill cut of the wind which powdered them with scooped-up puffs of snow. Dard watched the moon anxiously. No clouds to dim that. But clouds meant storm—and they dared not be caught in the open by a storm.

Kimber settled down to a lope which Dard found easy to match. How far they now were from the Cleft he had no way of knowing. And how long was it going to take them to get back? Did Kimber know the trail after they had to turn off the road? He himself might be able to find the path which led from the farm. But where was the farm?

"How far was your farm from that town?"

"About ten miles. But with all this snow—" Dard's breath made a white cloud about his head.

"Yes—the snow. And maybe more of it later. Look here, kid, this is the important part. We haven't too much time—"

"They may wait until morning to trail us. And if they bring dogs—"

"I don't mean that!" It appeared to Dard that Kimber waved away the idea of pursuit as if that did not matter. "This is what counts. The course the Voice set for us—I asked before we left how long it was good for. The answer was five days and two hours. Now I figure we have about five days and forty-five minutes. We have a blast off within that time or try a second visit to the Voice. Frankly, I think that would be hopeless."

"Five days and forty-five minutes," Dard echoed. "But, even if we have luck all the way it might take two—three days to reach the Cleft. And we haven't supplies—"

"Let us hope Kordov has kept things moving there," was Kimber's only comment. "And waiting here now isn't adding to our time. Come on."

Twice through the hours which followed they took to cover as 'copters went over. The machines ranged with an angry intentness in a circle and it hardly seemed possible that the fugitives could escape notice. But maybe it was their white clothing which kept them invisible.

The sun was up when Dard caught at the end of a time-eaten post projecting from the snow, swinging around to face the track it marked.

"Our farm lane," he bit off the words with economy as he rocked on his feet. To have made it this far—so soon. The 'copter must have taken them a good distance from town before it failed.

"Sure it is your place?"

Dard nodded, wasting no breath.

"Hmm." Kimber studied the unbroken white. "Prints on that are going to show up as well as ink. But no help for it."

"I wonder. The place was burnt—no supplies to be found there."

"Got a better suggestion?" Kimber's face was drawn and gaunt now."

"Folley's."

"But I thought—"

"Folley's dead. He ran the place with three work slaves. His son was tapped as a Peaceman recruit a month ago.

Suppose we were to smarten up and just tramp in. Say that our 'copter broke down in the hills and we walked in to get help—"

Kimber's eyes snapped alive. "And that does happen to these lame brains often enough. How many might be at the farm?"

"Folley's second wife, his daughter, the work slaves. I don't think he got an overseer after his son left."

"And they'd be only too willing to help Peacemen in distress! But they'll know you—"

"I've never seen Folley's wife—we didn't visit. And Lotta—well, she let me go before. But it's a better chance than trying to get into the mountains from here."

They tramped on, in the open now. And, at the end of Folley's lane, they reversed their jackets, shaking off what they could of the snow. They were still disheveled but a 'copter failure should account for that.

"After all," Kimber pointed out as they climbed the slight rise to the ugly farmhouse, "Peacemen don't explain to landsmen. If we ask questions and don't volunteer much we'll only be acting in character. It all depends on whether they've heard about the chase—"

Smoke arose from the chimney and Dard did not miss the betraying twitch at one of the curtains in a window facing the lane. The arrival was known. Lotta—everything depended now upon Lotta. He shot a glance at Kimber. All the good humor and amusement were wiped from that dark face. This was a tough—very tough muscle-boy, a typical Peaceman who would have no nonsense from a landsman.

The door on the porch which ran the side length of the house opened before they had taken two steps along the cleaned boards. A woman waited for them, her hands tugging smooth a food-spattered apron, an uneasy half-smirk spreading her lips to display a missing front tooth.

"Pax, noble sirs—Pax." Her voice was as fat and oily as her body and sounded more assured than her expression.

Kimber sketched a version of the official salute and

rapped out an answering "Pax—" in an authority-heavy tone. "This is—?"

Grotesquely she bobbed in an attempt at a curtsey. "The farm of Hew Folley, noble sir."

"And where is this Folley?" Kimber asked as if he expected the missing landsman to spring up before him.

"He is dead, sir. Murdered by outlaws. I thought that was why— But come in, noble sirs, come in—" She waddled back a step leaving the entrance to the kitchen open.

The rich smell of food caught at Dard's throat, until, for a second, he was almost nauseated. There were thick dishes on the stained table, and congealed grease, a fragment of bread, a half cup of herb tea, marked the remains of a late breakfast.

Without answering the woman's half-question Kimber seated himself on the nearest chair and with an outstretched arm swept the used dishes from before him. Dard dropped down opposite to the pilot, thankful for the support the hard wooden seat gave his trembling body.

"You have food, woman?" Kimber demanded. "Get it. We have been walking over this forsaken country for hours. Is there a messenger here we can send into town? Our 'copter is down and we must have the repair crew."

She was busy at the stove, breaking eggs, real eggs into a greasy skillet.

"Food, yes, noble sirs. But a messenger—since my man is dead I have only the slaves, and they are under lock and key. There is no one to send."

"You have no son?" Kimber helped himself to a piece of bread.

Her nervous smirk stretched to a smile. "Yes, noble sir, I have a son. But only this month he was chosen by the House of the Olive Branch. He is now in training for your own service, noble sir."

If she expected this information to unbend her visitors and soften their manners she was disappointed for Kimber merely raised his eyebrows before he continued:

"We can't walk to town ourselves, woman. Have you no one at all you can send?"

"There is Lotta." She went to the door and called the girl's name harshly. "With Hew gone she must see to the cows. But it is a long walk to town, noble sir."

"Then ride—or how *do* you get there when you go woman?" Kimber slid three eggs onto his plate and pushed the still laden platter over to Dard, who, a little dazed by the sight of such a wealth of food, made haste to help himself before it vanished.

"There is the colt. She might ride," the woman agreed reluctantly.

"Then let her get to it. I don't intend to sit out the whole of this day waiting for help. The sooner she goes, the better!"

"You want me?"

Dard knew that voice. For a long moment he dared not look up. But that inner compulsion which made him always face danger squarely raised his eyes to meet those of the girl standing in the half-open door. His fingers curled around the handle of the fork and bent it a trifle. But Lotta's stolid expression did not change and he could only hope that his own face was as blank.

"You want me?" she repeated.

The woman nodded at the two Peacemen. "These gentlemen—their 'copter broke down. They want you should take a message to town for them. Git the colt out and ride."

"All right." The girl tramped out and slammed the door behind her.

7. BATTLE AT THE BARRIER

Dard chewed mechanically on food which now had no savor. As Kimber forked a thick slice of ham he spoke to the pilot:

"Shall I give the girl instructions, sir?"

Kimber swallowed. "Very well. Be sure she gets it straight. I don't propose to sit around here waiting for a couple of days. Let her tell the repair master they may find us at the 'copter. We'll go back there after we thaw out. But get her started right away—the sooner she leaves the sooner they will come for us."

Dard went out into the farmyard. Lotta was saddling a horse. As his boots squeaked on the snow she looked up. "Where's Dessie? Wotta you done with her?"

"She's safe."

Lotta studied his face before she nodded. "That's the truth, ain't it? You really want I should go to town? Why? You ain't no Peaceman—"

"No. And the more you can delay your trip in, the better. But Lotta—" he had to give her some protection. If later she were suspected of aiding their escape her fate would not be pleasant. "When you get in and report at the Temple, tell them you are suspicious of us. We'll be gone from here by then."

With her chin she pointed to the house. "Don't you trust her none. She ain't my ma—Folley wasn't really my pa, neither. My pa was kin and Folley, he wanted the land pa left so they took me in. Don't you trust her none at all—she's worse'n Folley was. I'll ride slow goin' in, and I'll do like you say when I git there. Lissen here, Dard, you sure Dessie's gonna be all right?"

"She is if we can get back to her. She'll have a chance to live the way she ought to—"

The small eyes in the girl's pasty face were shrewd. "And that's a promise! You git outta here and take her too. I'll make up a good story for 'em. I ain't," she suddenly smiled at him, "I ain't near as dumb as I look, Dard Nordis, even if I ain't one of your kind!"

She scrambled awkwardly into the saddle and slapped the ends of the reins so that the horse broke into a trot.

Dard went back to the house and sat down at the table with a better appetite. Kimber broke off man-sized bites of apple tart, and between them he addressed his junior.

"Now that it's day, I've been thinking that we may be

able to check the bus over ourselves. You, woman," he said to their unwilling hostess, "can you direct them on to join us if we don't return?"

Dard pressured Kimber's foot with the toe of his boot in warning. And received a return nudge of acknowledgement.

"Which way you goin'?" she asked. Dard thought that some of her deference was gone. Was she beginning to suspect that she was not really entertaining two of the new lords of the land?

"North. We'll leave a trail, have to back track on your own. Suppose you put us up some grub so we'll have something at noon. And just send the repair crew along."

"Yes, noble sirs."

But that acknowledgement was almost grudging and she was spending a long time putting aside some pieces of cold meat and bread. Or did his jumpy nerves make him imagine that, wondered Dard.

A half hour later they left the house. They kept to the lane and then to the road leading north until a grove cut off their path from any watcher. It was then that Kimber faced west.

"Where now?"

"There's a trail farther on that doubles back up into the hills," Dard informed him. "It cuts across the old woods road near that tree where I met Sach."

"Good. I leave the guide duty up to you. But let's move! That girl may make a quick trip in—"

"She'll delay all she can. She knows—"

Kimber's lips shaped a soundless whistle. "That will help —if she is working for us."

"I told her that it meant saving Dessie. Dessie's the only one she cares about."

The warmth, good food, and short rest they had had at Folley's gave them heat and strength for the trail ahead. After two false tries Dard found the woods road. Along it there was an earlier trail breaking the snow, made by Lotta, he guessed.

Kimber set an easy pace, knowing the grueling miles

which still lay ahead. They took a lengthy rest at the rude lean-to by the message tree. The woods were unnaturally still and the sun reflected from patches of snow, making them squint against the glare.

From the message tree on, it was a matter of following the traces he himself had helped to make. Luckily, Dard congratulated himself, there had been no more snow and the broken path was easy to follow. But both were tired and slowed against their will as they slogged their way toward the heights which held the cave. There they could rest, Dard promised his aching body. They paused to eat, to breathe, and then on and on and on. Dard lost all track of time, it was a business of following in a robot fashion those other marks in the snow.

They had reached the lower slopes of the rise which would take them to the cave when he leaned against a tree. Kimber's face, stark and drawn, all the easy good humor pounded out of it by fatigue, was in outline against a snowbank.

It was in that moment of silence that Dard caught the distant sound—very faint, borne to them by some freak of air current—the bay of a hunting dog running a fresh and uncomplicated trail. Kimber's head jerked up. Dard ran his tongue around a dry mouth. That cave up there with its narrow entrance! He wasted no breath on explanation, instead he began doggedly to climb.

But—there was something wrong about the stone before them. Maybe his eyes—snow blindness—Dard shook his head, trying to clear them. But that different look remained. So that he was partly expecting what he found when he reached the crest. Sick, shaken to the point of nausea, he stared at the closed door of the cave—closed with rocks and something else—and then he reeled retching to the other side of the hill top.

He was scrubbing out his mouth with a handful of snow when Kimber joined him.

"So, now we know about Sach—"

Dard raised sick eyes. The pilot's mouth was stone-hard. "Left him there like that as a threat," muttered Kimber, "and a warning. They must have discovered that this was one of our regular posts."

"How could any one do that?"

"Listen, son, somebody starts out with an idea—maybe in the beginning a good one. Renzi wasn't a crook, he was basically a decent man. I heard his early speeches and I'm willing to agree that much he said was true. But he had no—well, 'charity' is the best word for it. He wanted to force his pattern for living on everyone else, for their own good, of course. Because he was great and sincere in his own way he gained a following of honest people. They were sick of war and they were terribly shocked by the Big Burn, they could readily believe that science had led to evil. The Free Scientists were too independent—they made closed guilds of their teams. There was a separation between thinking and feeling. And feeling is easier to us than thinking. So Renzi appealed to feeling, and against the aloofness of science he won. He was joined by other fanatics, and by those who want power no matter how it comes into their hands. Then there has always been some human beings who enjoy that sort of thing—what we just saw over there. They're lower than animals because animals don't torture their own kind for pleasure. Fanatics, power lovers, sadists—let them get a tight hold on the government and there is no room for decency. The best this world can hope for now is a break in their ranks, an inner struggle for control.

"This type of fight against freedom of thought and tolerance has happened before. Centuries ago there was the Inquisition in the name of religion. And during the twentieth century the dictators did the same under political systems of one kind or another. Fanatic belief in an idea—a conviction that an idea or a nation is greater than the individual man—it has scrounged us again and again. Utter power over his fellow men changes a man, rots him through and through. When we are able to breed men who want no influence over each other—who are content to strive equally for a common goal—then we'll pull ourselves above that—" He gestured to that pitiful thing now hidden

78

from their eyes. "The Free Scientists came close to reaching that point. Which is why Renzi and his kind both hated and feared them. But they were only a handful—drops lost in a sea. And they went under as have others before them who have followed the same vision. Nothing worse can be done to man than what he has done to himself. But listen to this—"

Kimber's head was high, he was watching that peak which guarded the distant Cleft. Now he repeated slowly:

" 'Frontiers of any type, physical or mental, are but a challenge to our breed. Nothing can stop the questing of men, not even Man. If we will it, not only the wonders of space, but the very stars are ours!' "

"The stars are ours!" echoed Dard. "Who said that?"

"Techneer Vidor Chang, one of our martyrs. He helped to bring the star ship here, ventured out on the first fuel research and— But his words remain ours.

"That's what we've geared our lives to, we outlaws. It doesn't matter what a man was in the past—Free Scientist, techneer, laborer, farmer, soldier—we're all one because we believe in freedom for the individual, in the rights of man to grow and develop as far as he can. And we are daring to search for a place where we can put those beliefs into practice. The earth denied us—we must seek the stars."

Kimber started down slope. Dard caught up to point out the ruse which he had used with Dessie and which might now baffle the hounds. They found a higher ledge and made a more perilous dive, so that Dard landed on pine boughs and spilled to the earth with a jolt which drove the breath out of his lungs until Kimber pounded air back into him.

To his surprise the pilot did not keep to cover now. The night was falling fast and they could not hold their present pace without rest. But Kimber plunged on until they came to the open space flanking the river. There the pilot brought out the same flat disc with which he had cut their way out of the temple barrier, and hurled it out into the open.

A column of green fire shot from it up into the night, standing steady for at least five minutes. In the dusk it made a good show, turning the surrounding snow and the faces of the fugitives verdant as it burned.

"Now we wait," Kimber's voice held a faint shadow of the old humor. "The boys will be down to pick us up before Fax can connect."

But waiting was not so simple when each minute meant the difference between life and death. They swallowed the last of the food and bedded down between two fallen trees at the edge of the clearing. The flame died down, but a core of green glow would continue to shine for several hours, Kimber said.

A wind was rising. And its wails through the trees did not drown out the distant yapping of the hounds. Dard fingered his stun gun—two charges for him, one in Kimber's weapon. Little enough with which to meet what panted on their trail. The trailers would be armed with rifles.

Kimber stirred and then scuttled on hands and feet out from their shelter. From the night sky a dark shape came down—a 'copter. But the pilot summoned Dard to meet with it. A door opened and he was shoved into the machine by his companion. Then as they were air borne Dard rested his head against a cushion, only half hearing the excited questions and answers of the others.

When he awoke the whole wild adventure of the past forty-eight hours might only have been a dream, for he was back on the same cot where he had rested before. Only now Kimber was not with him. Dard lay there, try-ing to separate dream from reality. Then a clang which could only have been an alarm brought him up. With clumsy hands he pulled on the clothes lying in a heap on the floor and opened the door to peer out into the corridor.

Two men, pushing before them a small cart, crossed its lower end. The cart wheel caught on the edge of a doorway and both men cursed as they worked swiftly to pry it loose. Dard padded in that direction, but before he could join them they were gone. He followed as they broke into a trot and started down a ramp leading into the heart of the mountain.

This brought them to a large cave which was a scene of complete confusion. Dard hesitated, trying to pick out of the busy throng some familiar face. There were two parties at work. One was carrying and wheeling boxes and containers out into the narrow valley where the star ship was berthed. And in this group women toiled with the men. The second party, which had been joined b, the men with the cart, was wholly masculine and all armed.

"Hey, you!"

Dard realized that he was being hailed by a black-bearded man using a rifle as a baton to direct the movements of the armed force. He went over there, only to have a rifle thrust into his hands and to be urged into line with the men taking a tunnel to the right. They were bound for a defense point, he decided, but no one explained.

The answer came soon enough with a crackle of rifle fire. What had once been the narrow throat-valley leading into the Cleft proper had been choked up by a fall of tumbled rock and earth cemented by snow, broken in places by the protruding crown or roots of a small tree. Up this dam men were crawling, dragging after them an assortment of weapons, from ordinary rifles and stun guns to a tube and box arrangement totally strange to Dard.

He counted at least ten defenders who were now ensconced in hollows along the rim of the barrier. Now and again one of these fired, the sound being echoed by the rock walls to twice its normal volume. Dard clambered over the slide, cautiously testing his footing, until he reached the nearest of the snipers' hollows. The man glanced up as a rolling clod announced his arrival.

"Get your fool head down, kid!" he snapped. "They're still trying the 'copter game. You'd think that they'd have learned by now!"

Dard wormed his way along until he rubbed shoulders with the defender and could look down into the weird battlefield. He tried to piece out from the wreckage there what had been happening in the hours since he and Kimber had returned.

Two burnt-out skeletons of 'copters were crumpled among rocks. From one of them thin wisps of vapor still spiraled. And there were four bodies wearing black and white Pax livery. But as far as Dard could see there was nothing alive down there now.

"Yeah. They've all taken t' cover. Trying to think up some trick that'll get us away from here. It'll take time for 'em to get any big guns back in these hills. And they don't have time. Before they can shake us loose the ship's going to blast off!"

"The ship's going to blast off!" So that was it! He was now one of an expendable rear guard, left to hold the fort while the star ship won free. Dard studied the rifle he held, with eyes which did not see either the metal of barrel or wood of stock.

Well, he told himself savagely, wasn't this just what he knew was going to happen—ever since that moment when Kimber had admitted with his silence that all those in the Cleft would not go out into space?

"Hey!" a hand joggling his elbow snapped his attention back to the job at hand. "See—down there——"

He followed the line set by that dirty finger. Something moved around the wreckage of the 'copter farthest from the barrier—a black tube. Dard frowned as he studied its outline. The tube was being slued around to face the barrier. That was no rifle—too large. It was no form of gun he had seen before.

"Santee! Hey, Santee!" his companion shouted. "They're bringing up a burper!"

A man scrambled up and Dard was shoved painfully against a tree branch as the black beard took his place.

"You're right—damn it! I didn't think they had any of those left! Well, we've got to stay as long as we can. I'll pass the word to the boys. In the meantime try a little ricochet work. Might pick off one or two of that beauty's crew. If we're lucky. Which I'm beginning to think now we certainly ain't!"

He crawled out of the hollow and Dard got thankfully back into station. His companion patted down a ridge of dirt on which to rest the barrel of his rifle. Dard saw that he was aiming, not at the ugly black muzzle of the burper, but at the rock wall behind the gun. So—that was what Santee meant by ricochet work! Fire at the rock wall and hope that the bullets would be deflected back against the men serving the burper. Neat—if it could be done. Dard lined the sights of his own weapon to cover what he hoped was the proper point. Others had the same idea. The shots came in a ragged volley. And the trick worked, for with a scream a man reeled out and fell.

"Why don't they use that green gas?" asked Dard, remembering his own introduction to the fighting methods of the Cleft dwellers.

"How do you think we crashed those 'copters, kid? And the boys got a couple more machines the same way out by the river. Only something went wrong when they triggered the blast to seal off the valley this way. And the gas gun—with a couple of very good guys—came down with this—underneath!"

For a space the burper did not move. Perhaps the defenders had wiped out its crew with the ricochet volley. Just as they were beginning to hope that this was so, the black muzzle, moving with the ponderous slowness of some big animal, eased back into concealment. Dard's partner watched this maneuver sourly.

"Cookin' up something else now. They must have had a guy with brains come in to run things. And if that's so, we're not going to have it so good. Yahh!" His voice arose sharply.

But Dard needed no warning. He, too, had seen that black sphere rising in a lazy course straight at the barrier.

"Head down, kid! Head——"

Dard burrowed into the side of the hollow, his face scratching across the frozen dirt, his hunched shoulders and arms protecting his head. The explosion rocked the ground and was followed by a scream and several moans. Dazed, the boy shook himself free of loose earth and snow.

To the left there was a sizeable gap in the barrier. With a white patch halfway down—not snow but a hand buried to the wrist in the slide the explosion had ripped down.

"Dan—and Red—and Loften got it. Nice bag for Pax," his fellow sniper muttered. "Now was that just a lucky shot—or do they have our range?"

The forces of Pax had the range. A second ragged tear was sliced across the rock and earth dam. Before the stones stopped rattling down, Dard was shaken out of his crouch roughly.

"If you ain't dead, kid, come on! Santee's passed the word to fall back, to the next turn of the canyon. On the double, because we're going to blow again, and if you get caught on this side—it's your skin!"

Dard tumbled down the barrier behind his guide, falling once and scraping both sleeve and skin from his forearm in the process. Seconds later eight defenders, their sides heaving, their dirty faces haunted and drawn, gathered around Santee and were waved on down the canyon. Santee himself stood counting off seconds aloud. At "ten" he plunged his hand down on the black box beside him.

There was a dull rumble, less noise than the burper shots had made. Dard watched in a sort of fascinated horror as the whole opposite cliff moved majestically outward into space before it crashed down to make a second and taller wall. The stones and earth had not ceased to roll before Santee was leading his force up it to dig in and face the enemy. Once more Dard lay in wait with a rifle, this time alone.

The burper sounded regularly, systematically pounding down the first barrier. But, save for that, there was no sign of Pax activity. And how long would it be before they brought the burper up to this assault? Then would the few left retreat again and blow down another section of the mountain?

There was a flicker of movement down at the first barrier, and it was answered by a shot from the defense. A second later more shots, all down by the battered dam. Dard guessed what had happened, wounded and left behind, one of the Cleft dwellers was firing his last round to delay the victors. The flurry of fire was only a prelude to what they were waiting to see—the black snub nose of the burper rising above the rubble.

8. COLD SLEEP

UNABLE TO SEE the burper's crew the defenders had only the narrowest and most impossible mark to shot at—the gun's muzzle. Perhaps that action was only to occupy their minds, by concentrating on that menace, by seeing or thinking of nothing else, they could, each and everyone, forget for a space that the ship they fought for could only take a numbered few—that when it blasted off, some of the Cleft would still be here.

Dessie! Dard twisted in the hole he had hollowed with his body. Surely Dessie would be aboard. There were so few children—so few women—Dessie would be an asset!

He tried to think only of a shadow he thought he saw move then. Or a shadow he wanted to believe had moved as he snapped a shot at it. When this battle had begun, or rather when he had come on the scene—it had been mid-morning. Once during the day he had choked down some dry food which had been passed along, taking sips from a shared canteen. Now the dusk of evening lengthened the patches of gloom. Under the cover of the dark the burper would rumble up to them, to gnaw away at this second barrier. And the defenders would withdraw—to delay and delay.

But maybe the end of that battle would not wait upon nightfall after all. The familiar sound of blades beating the air was a warning which reached them before they saw the 'copter skimming up, its undercarriage scraping the top of their first wall.

Dard watched it resignedly, too apathetic to duck when its occupants hurled grenades. He crouched unmoving as the machine climbed for altitude. The explosion caught him in his hollow a second later. There was the sense of being torn out of hiding, of being flung free. Then he was on his hands and knees, creeping through a strangely silent world of rolling stones and sliding earth.

Some feet away a man struggled to free his legs from a mound of earth. He clawed at his covering with a single hand, the other, welling red, lay at a queer twisted angle. Dard crept over and the man stared at him wildly, mouthing words Dard could not hear through the buzzing which filled his head. He dug with torn fingers into the mass which held the other prisoner.

Another figure loomed over them and Dard was shoved aside. The huge Santee knelt, scooping away soil and rock, until together they were able to pull the injured man free. Dard, his shaking head still ringing with noise of its own, helped to lift the limp body and carry it back into the inner valley of the star ship. Santee stumbled and brought all three of them down. Dard got to his knees and turned his head carefully to blink at what he saw behind him.

Those in the 'copter had not ripped apart the barrier as they had planned. The grenades had jarred some hidden fault bringing down more tons of soil and rocks. Anyone viewing that spot now would never believe that there had once been an opening there.

Of the defenders who had held that barricade only the three of them remained—he, Santee, and the wounded man they had dragged with them.

Dard wondered if he had been deafened by the explosion. The roaring in his head, which affected his balance when he tried to walk, had no connection with normal sound and he could hear nothing Santee was saying. He ran his hands aimlessly across his bruised and aching ribs, content to remain where he was.

But the enemy was not satisfied to leave them alone. Spurts of dust stung up from the rock wall. Dard stared at them a second or two before Santee's heavy fist sent him sprawling, and he realized that the three of them were cut off in a pocket while snipers in the 'copter tried to pick them off. This was the end—but to think that brought him no sensation of fear. It was enough to just lie still and wait.

He brought his hands up to support his buzzing head. Then someone tugged roughly at his belt, rolling him over. Dard opened his eyes to see Santee taking the stun gun from him. Out of that thick mat of black hair which masked most of the man's face his teeth showed in a white snarl of rage.

But there were only two charges in the stun gun. Maybe he was able to say that aloud, for Santee glanced at him and then examined the clip. Two shots from a stun gun wasn't going to bring down a 'copter. The humor of that pricked him and he laughed quietly to himself. A stun gun against a 'copter!

Santee was up on his knees behind the rock he had chosen for protection, his head straining back on his thick neck as he watched the movements of the copter.

What happened next might have astonished Dard earlier, but now he was past all amazement. The 'copter, making a wide turn, smashed into some invisible barrier in the air. Through the twilight they saw it literally bounce back, as if some giant hand had slapped at an annoying insect. Then, broken as the insect would have been, it came tumbling down. Two of its passengers jumped and floated through the air, supported by some means Dard could not identify. Santee scrambled to his feet and took careful aim with the stun gun.

He picked off the nearer. But a second shot missed the other. And the big man ducked only just in time to escape the return fire of the enemy. Making contact with the ground the Peaceman dodged behind the crumpled fuselage of the 'copter. Why didn't he just walk across and finish them off, Dard speculated fretfully. Why draw out the process? It was getting darker—darker. He pawed at his eyes, was his sight as well as his hearing going to fail him?

But, no, he could still see Santee who had gone down on his belly and was now wriggling around the rocks, proceeding worm-fashion along a finger of the slide toward the 'copter. Though how he expected to attack the man hidden there—with his bare hands and an empty stun gun—against a rifle!

Dard's detachment persisted. He watched the action in which he was not involved critically. Wanting to see how it would end he pulled himself up to follow Santee's slow progress. When the crawler disappeared from his range of vision Dard was irritated. Suppose the man waiting over there was to believe that they were trying to escape down valley—wouldn't all his attention be for that direction—not at Santee?

Dard felt about him in the gloom, hunting stones of a suitable size, weighing and discarding until he held one larger than both his fists. Two more he lined up before him. With all the strength he could muster he sent the first and largest hurling down the valley. A flash of fire answered its landing.

The second and third rock followed at intervals. Each time he saw the mark of answering shots. His hearing was coming back—he caught the faint echo of the last one. New stones were found and sent after the others—to keep up the illusion of escape. But now there was no shot to reply. Had Santee reached that sniper?

The boy sprawled back against the wall of the cleft and waited, for what he did not altogether know. Santee's return? Or the star ship's blast off? Had they brought time enough for the frenzied workers back there? Was tonight going to see Kimber setting that course they had won from the Voice, piloting the ship out into space before he, too, went under the influence of Lars' drug and began the sleep from which there might be no awakening? But if the voyagers did awaken! Dard drew a deep breath and for a moment he forgot everything—his own aching, punished body, the rocky trap which enclosed him, the lack of future —he forgot all these in a dream of what might lie beyond the sky which he now searched for the first wink of star-light. Another world—another sun—a fresh start!

He started as a shape loomed out of the dark to cut off the sight of that star he had just discovered. Fingers clawed painfully into his shoulders bringing him up to his feet. Then, mainly by Santee's brute force of body and will, they picked up the rescued man and started in a drunken stagger back into the valley. Dard forgot his dream, he needed all his strength to keep his feet, to go as Santee drove him.

They made a half-turn to avoid a boulder and came to a stop as lights blinded them. The ship was surrounded by a circle of blazing flares. The fury of industry which had boiled about it during the loading had stemmed to a mere trickle. Dard could see no women at all and most of the men were gone also. The few who remained in sight were passing boxes up a ramp. Soon that would be done, and then those down there would enter that silvery shape. The hatch would close, the ship would rise on fire.

Muted by the pain in his head he heard the booming shout of a deep voice. Below, the loaders stopped work. Grouped together they faced the survivors of the barrier battle. Santee called again, and that group broke apart as the men ran up to them.

Dard sat down beside the injured man, his legs giving way under him. With detachment he watched the coming of that other party. One man had his shirt badly torn across the shoulder—would he land on another world across the void of space with that tatter still fluttering? The problem had some interest.

Now a circle of legs walled the boy in, boots spurted snow in his face. He was brought to his feet, arms about his shoulders, led along to the ship. But that wasn't right, he thought mistily. Kimber had said not room enough—he was one of the expendables——

But he could find no words to argue with those who helped him along, not even when he was pushed up that ramp into the ship. Kordov stood in the hatch door waving them ahead with an imperious arm. Then Dard found himself in a tiny room and a cup of milky liquid was thrust against his lips and held there until he docilely swallowed its contents to the last tasteless drop. When that was in him he was lowered onto a folding seat pulled down from the starkly bare metal wall and left to hold his spinning head in his hands.

"Yeah—the force field's still holdin'——"

"Won't be able to plow through that last slide, eh?"

"Not with anything they've got now."

Words, a lot of words, passing pack and forth across him. Sometimes for a second or two they made good sense, then meaning faded again.

"Can pretty well take your own time now——" Was that rumble from Santee?

And that quick, crisp voice cutting in, "What about the kid?"

"Him? He's some scrapper. Got a head on him, too. Just shaken up a lot when that last blowup hit us, but he's still in one piece."

Kimber! That had been Kimber asking about him. But Dard hadn't strength left to raise his head and look for the pilot.

"We'll patch up Tremont first and send him under. You two will have to wait a while. Give them the soup and that first powder, Lui——"

Again Dard was given a drink—this time of hot steamy stuff which carried the flavor of rich meat. After it there was a capsule to be swallowed.

Bruises and aches—when he moved his body he was just one huge ache. But he straightened up and tried to take an interest in his surroundings. Santee, his shirt a few rags about his thick hairy shoulders and arms, squatted on another pull-down seat directly across from Dard. Along the passage outside there was a constant coming and going. Scraps of conversation reached them, most of which he did not understand.

"Feelin' better, kid?" the big man asked.

Dard answered that muffled question with a nod and then wished that he hadn't moved his head.

"Are we going along?" he shaped the words with difficulty.

Santee's beard wagged as he roared with laughter. "Like to see 'em throw us off ship now! What made you think we weren't, kid?"

"No room—Kimber said."

Laughter faded from the eyes of the man opposite him.

"Might not have been, kid. Only a lot of good men died back there puttin' such a plug in the valley that these buggers aren't going to git in 'til too late. Since the warp's still workin', flyin' won't bring 'em neither. So we ain't needed out there no more. An' maybe some good fightin' men *will* be needed where this old girl's headed. So in we come, an' they're gonna pack us away with the rest of the cargo. Ain't that so, Doc?" he ended by demanding of the tall young man who had just entered.

The newcomer's parrot crest of blond hair stood up from his scalp in a twist like the stem of a pear and his wide eyes glowed with enthusiasm.

"You're young Nordis, aren't you?" he demanded of Dard, ignoring Santee. "I wish I could have known your brother! He—what he did——! I wouldn't have believed such results possible if I hadn't seen the formula! Hibernation and freezing—his formula combined with Tas's biological experiments! Why, we've even put three of Hammond's calves under—what grass they'll graze on before they die! And it's all due to Lars Nordis!"

Dard was too tired to show much interest in that. He wanted to go to sleep—to forget everything and everybody. *"To sleep, perchance to dream"*—the old words shaped patterns for him. Only—not to dream would be better now. Did one dream in space—and what queer dreams haunted men lying in slumber between worlds? Dard mentally shook himself—there was something important—something he had to ask before he dared let sleep come.

"Where's Dessie?"

"Nordis' little girl? She's with my daughter—and my wife —they're already under."

"Under what?"

"In cold sleep. Most of the gang are now. Just a few of us still loading. Then Kimber, Kordov and I. We'll ride out until Kimber is sure of the course before we stow away. All the rest of you——"

"Will be packed away before the take-off. Saves wear and tear on bodies and nerves under acceleration," cut in Kimber from the doorway. He nodded over the medico's shoulder at Dard. "Glad to have you aboard, kid. Promise you—no forced landings on this voyage. You're to be sealed up in crew's quarters—so you'll wake early to see the new world!" And with that he was gone again.

Maybe it was the capsule acting now, maybe it was just that last reassurance from a man he had come to trust wholeheartedly, but Dard was warm and relaxed. To wake and see a new world!

Santee went away with Lui Skort, and Dard was alone. The noise in the corridor died away. At last he heard a warning bell. And a moment later the pound of heavy feet in a hurry roused him. The haste of that spoke of trouble, and with the support of the wall he got up to look out. Kimber was coming down a spiral stairway, the center core of the ship. In his hand was one of the snubnosed ray guns Sach had had. He passed Dard without a word.

Bracing his hands against the wall of the corridor, Dard shuffled along in his wake. Then he was peering out of an airlock to see the pilot squatting on the ramp. It was black night out—most of the flares had gone out.

Dard listened. He could hear at intervals the blast of the burper. The Peacemen were still doggedly attacking the cleft barrier. But what had Kimber come to guard and why? Have some important possessions been left in the caverns? Dard slumped against the lock and watched lights spark to life in the mouth of the tunnel. A man came out running, covering the ground to the foot of the ship's ramp in ground-eating leaps. He dashed by Kimber, and Dard had just time enough to get back as Santee burst in.

"Get going!" The big man bore him along to the corridor and Kimber joined them. He touched some control and the hatch-lock was sealed.

Santee, panting, grinned. "Nice neat job, if I do say so myself," he reported. "The space warp's off an' the final charge is set for forty minutes from now. We'll blast before that?"

"Yes. Better get along both of you. Lui's waiting and we don't want to scrape a couple of acceleration cases off the floor later," returned Kimber.

With the aid of the other two Dard pulled his tired body up the stair, past various landing stages where sealed doors fronted them. Kordov's broad face appeared at last, surveying them anxiously, and it was he who lifted Dard up the last three steps. Kimber left them—climbing on through an opening above into the control chamber. He did not glance back or say any goodbyes.

"In here——" Kordov thrust them ahead of him.

Dard, brought face to face with what that cabin contained, knew a sudden repulsion. Those boxes, shelved in a metal rack—they too closely resembled coffins! And the rack was full except for the bottommost box which awaited open on the floor.

Kordov pointed to it. "That's for you, Santee—built for a big boy. You're lighter, Dard. We'll fit you in on top over on the other side."

A second rack stood against the farther wall with four more of the coffins ready and waiting. Dard shivered, but it was not imagination—disturbed nerves which roughened his skin, there was a chill in the air—coming from the open boxes.

Kordov explained. "You go to sleep and then you freeze."

Santee chuckled. "Just so you thaw us out again, Tas. I ain't aimin' to spend the rest of my life an icicle, so you brainy boys can prove somethin' or other. Now what do we do—climb in?"

"Strip first," ordered the First Scientist. "And then you get a couple of shots."

He pulled along a small rolling tray-table on which were laid a series of hypodermics. Carefully he selected two, one filled with a red brown liquid, the other with a colorless substance.

93

As Dard fumbled at the fastenings of the torn uniform he still wore, Santee asked a question for them both.

"An' how do we wake up when the right time comes? Got any alarms set in these contraptions?"

Those three—" Kordov indicated the three lower coffins on the far rack, "are especially fitted. Arranged to waken those inside, Kimber, Lui, and me, when the ship signals that it has reached the end of the course set, which will be when the intruments raise a sun enough like Sol to nourish earth-type planets. We feed that into her robot controls once we are free in space. During the voyage she may vary the pattern—to make evasion of meteors or for other reasons. But she will always come back on the set course. If we are close to a solar system when we are awakened, and Kimber has done everything possible to assure that, then we shall arouse you others needed to bring the ship down. Most of you won't be awakened until after we land—there isn't enough room."

Kordov shrugged, "Who knows? No man has yet pioneered into the galaxy. It may be for generations."

Santee rolled his discarded clothing into a ball and waited stoically for Kordov to give him the shots. Then with a wave of one big fist he climbed into the coffin and lay down. Kordov made adjustments at either end. Icy air welled up in a freezing puff. Santee's eyes closed as the First Scientist moved the lid into place before setting the three dials on the side. Their pointers swung until the needles came to rest at the far end. Kordov pushed the box back onto the rack.

"Now for you," he turned to Dard.

The top box lowered itself on two long arms from the top of the other rack. Dard discarded his last piece of clothing with a vast reluctance. Sure, he could understand the theory of this—what his brother had worked out for them. But the reality—to be frozen within a box—to go sightlessly, helplessly into the void—perhaps never to awake! With his teeth set hard he fought back the panic those thoughts churned up in him. And he was fighting so hard that the prick of the first injection came as a shock. He started, only to have Kordov's hand close as a vise upon his upper arm and hold him steady for a second.

"That's all—in with you now, son. See you in another world."

Kordov was laughing, but Dard's weak answering smile as he settled himself in the coffin had no humor in it. Because Kordov could be so very right. The cover was going on, he had an insane desire to scream out that he wasn't going to be shut in this way—that he wanted out, not only of the box, but of the whole crazy venture. But the lid was on now. It was cold—so cold—dark—cold. This was space as man had always believed it would be—cold and dark—eternal cold and dark—without end.

BOOK TWO

ASTRA

1. AWAKENING

IT WAS WARM and there was a light, striking redly through Dard's closed eyelids. The warmth was good, but he wanted to twist his head away from the demands of that light. To move—but movement required effort he had not yet the strength to make. It would be better to slip back into the pleasant darkness—to sleep. . . .

A sharp stab of pain shook him out of that floating ease. Dard made a great effort and forced his eyelids up. Cloudy masses of color moved above him, sometimes changing position in quick jerks which removed them entirely from his area of vision. The cloudiness slowly disappeared and lines tightened, drew together. A face—vaguely familiar—hands which descended to his level of sight.

He became aware of the hands moving across his body and another prick of pain followed. There was sound—staccato bursts. Talking—talking—Dard willed his mouth to open, his tongue to move. But obedience came with agonizing slowness, as if those particular motions had not been made for a long, long time. How long? Long—? He began to remember, and his hands turned to feel for the confines of the coffin. But they met no barrier—he was no longer imprisoned in that box!

"Drink up, kid——"

The words sorted themselves into coherent speech as he sucked on the tube which had been placed in his mouth.

96

The drink was hot, warmth tingling inside him as well as without, driving the chill which had immobilized his muscles. Strangely he was drowsy again and this time the hands did not work to keep him conscious.

"That's right. Take it easy—we'll be seeing you. . . ."

That reassurance carried into sleep with him. It held through to his second awakening. This time he raised himself up and looked around. He had been stretched on a soft thick pad on the floor of the oddest room he had ever seen. Half lying in a cushioned chair swung on webbing was a dark-haired man, intent upon a wide screen set in the wall before him.

There were two more such seats, each before a board of controls. And Dard saw three more such floor mats as the one he rested upon, each equipped with a set of straps and buckles. He drew his feet up under him to sit cross-legged, while he studied the cabin and put together bits of recollection.

This could not be anything but the control cabin of the star ship. He was awake—had been aroused—which meant ——! His hand went to his mouth in an involuntary gesture. Now he wanted to see what was on that screen his cabin companion watched. He must see!

But his body moved so slowly. Rusty joints—slack muscles. Why—he creaked! Hands and eyes told him that he was clothed. Though the cloth of the breeches and blouse was sleek and smooth, like no other fabric he had ever seen, colored in a mixture of brown and green. He put out the feet in their queer soft boots and inched forward to grab at the nearest swinging chair.

The watcher turned his head and smiled. It was Kimber —the same Kimber he had last seen on his way to this cabin on the night the voyage had begun. How long ago had that been?

"Greetings!" The pilot pointed to the chair beside his own. "Sit down—you haven't got your ship's legs yet. Did you have good dreams?"

Dard moved his tongue experimentally. "Can't remember any," the words came out easily now—at least his voice hadn't rusted away. "Where are we?"

Kimber chuckled. "Space only knows. But we're near enough to a reasonable goal for the old girl to awake Kordov and me. Then we added you to the company—and will probably bring around a couple more before we land. See?"

On the screen three specks of light dotted the dark glass.

"That's it, a new solar system, m'boy! Luck—Lord, Luck's ridden on our rockets most of the way. That"—Kimber pointed to the largest of the dots—"that is a yellow sun, approximate temperature 11,000 degrees, approximate size—same as Sol. In fact, it could be Sol's twin brother. And being Sol's twin we can hope that one of its three planets is enough like Terra to make us welcome."

"Three planets—I only see two."

"Other's behind Sol II now. We've seen her—in fact Tas and I have had a week to chart this system since the ship controls roused us. Give us another day and we shall pick out the world we want and land the ship——"

Three worlds—and a yellow sun. Dard wished that he knew more, that his education was better than a collection of scraps and patches. Back on earth under Pax it was a feat to be able to read and write—he had entertained some pride in his learning. But now—he felt that to be nothing at all!

"Why did you waken me?" he asked. "I can't help with the ship. You said that Kordov and you——" He was trying to remember. There had been a third man to be aroused early——

Kimber's attention was again given to the screen. Now he answered quickly:

"You were available and you can help Kordov. Lui didn't make it."

Lui Skort—that young medico who had been so enthusiastic about Lars' drug! *He* had been that third man.

"What—what happened?"

"We can't tell now. All of this—the ship, her course, the freeze boxes were constructed on hope alone. We had no way of testing anything properly. The ship awakened Kordov and me. But Lui——"

"How long have we been cruising in deep space?"

"At least three hundred years—maybe more. Time in space may be different from planet time. That is one of the points scientists have argued about. We have no accurate way of telling."

"Was it only Lui's box that failed?"

Kimber's face was grim now as it had been on that night they fought their way back to the Cleft.

"Until we land and start to rouse the whole company we can not tell. The freeze boxes must not be opened until their occupants are ready for revival. And the ship is too small to do that before landing——".

Coffins! Coffins were what they resembled, and coffins they might be for the whole inert cargo the star ship carried! Perhaps the three of them were the only survivors.

"We can hope for a high percentage of survivals," Kimber continued. "Lui's box had the special controls—that may have been the trouble. But out of four, three of us are all right. Kordov——"

"Yes—and what does Kordov do?" asked the hearty voice behind them.

The stocky First Scientist elbowed his way between the two swinging seats and handed the occupant of each a round plastic bulb from which a tube projected. He cradled a third in his own hand as he settled in the other chair.

"Kordov," he answered his own question, "continues to see after your puny bodies, my friends. And you should be glad of his personal interest in them. You will now consume what you hold in your paws and be thankful!" He inserted the bulb tube in his mouth and took a smacking suck.

Dard discovered that he had to drink the same warm salty stuff that had been given to him on his first awakening. And it satisfied him completely. But he only took one experimental drag before he demanded:

"I heard about Lui. How many others?"

Tas Kordov wiped his mouth with the back of his square hand.

"That we can not tell. We dare not investigate the boxes too closely until a landing has been made. Yes, all of us want an answer to that question, young man. How many——? We can hope that most came through. I propose to open two more from the crews' quarters—there are men in them whose skills we need. But—for the rest—their slumbers must continue until we have the new world to offer them. And that too," he waved at the visa-screen, "presents problems. We have found the proper sort of sun. But remember Sol had nine planets, on only one of which mankind could live at ease. Here are three planets—perhaps a Mars, a Venus, a Mercury, and no Terra. Which one do you think we should try, Sim?"

The pilot drank before he replied. "Judging by the charted orbits, I'll settle for the middle one. It's closer to Sol II than Terra was to Sol I, but it has the nearest approach to a Terran orbit."

"I don't know anything about astronomy," Dard ventured. "You expect this sun to produce an earth-type planet because it is a 'yellow' one, but if one of those three worlds *is* another Terra—what about intelligent life on it? Couldn't the same general conditions have produced the same type of dominant life form?"

Kordov leaned forward, disturbing the precarious balance of his swinging seat.

"Intelligent life—maybe. Humanoid of Man—only perhaps. If on one planet the primate is the ruling form, on another it may be the insect or the carnivora."

"Don't forget this!" Kimber held up one hand and flexed its fingers in front of the screen. "Man's hand helped to make him the ruling form. Suppose you had only—say, a cat's paw. Even if intelligence went with it, and I defy anyone to tell me that a cat is not an intelligent creature; its brains may work in a different pattern, perhaps, but no one who has lived with one can deny that it can alter its environment to suit its convenience, in spite of the general stupidity of the human beings that it must deal with and through. But if we had been born with paws instead of hands—no matter what super brains we had, could we have produced tools, or other artifacts? Primates on Terra had hands. And they used them to pull themselves up to a material civilization, just as they used monkey chatter and worse than monkey manners to break up what they themselves had created. No, if we had not possessed hands we would have achieved nothing."

"Very well," Kordov returned, "I grant you the advantage of hands. But I still say that some ruling species other than primates might well have developed under slightly different conditions. All history, both man-made and physical, is conditioned by 'ifs.' Suppose your super cats have learned to use their paws and are awaiting us. But this is romancing," he laughed. "Let us hope that what lies there is a world upon which intelligent life has never come into existence at all. If we are lucky——"

Kimber scowled at the screen. "Luck has ridden on our jets all the way. Sometimes I wonder if we have been a little too lucky and there's a rather nasty pay-off waiting for us right at the end of this voyage. But we can at least choose our landing place and I intend to set us down as far from any signs of civilization—if there is a civilization—as I can. Say in a desert or——"

"We shall leave the selection of the spot to you, Sim. And now, Dard, if you have finished your meal, you will please come with me. There is work to be done."

Dard's attempt to get to his feet unbalanced him and he would have fallen had it not been for the First Scientist.

"These cabins have some gravity," Kordov explained. "But not as much as we knew on Terra. Hold on and move slowly until you learn how to keep your feet."

Dard did as he advised, clutching at the chairs and anything within reach until he came to the round opening of the door. Beyond that was a much smaller cabin with two built-in bunks and a series of supply cupboards.

"This is pilot's quarters during an interplanetary run." Kordov crossed to the center of the room where a well-shaped opening gave access to the ship below. "Come on down——"

Dard gingerly descended the steep stair, coming into the section where he had been stored away for the cold sleep. And Kordov was going into that very cabin. The three boxes on the far rack were open. On the other rack the coffins were solidly white as if they had been carved from virgin snow.

Kordov pressed a button and the topmost box came down to the floor. He freed it from the arms which had lowered it and trundled his prize to the door with Dard's help. Together they brought the coffin into a second chamber which was a miniature laboratory. Kordov went down on his knees to read the dials. After a minute inspection he sighed with relief.

"It is well. Now we shall open——"

The lid resisted as if ages of time had applied a stiff glue. But under continued pressure it gave at last with a faint swish of air. Crisp cold curled up about them, bringing with it chemical scents. The First Scientist examined the stiff body in the exposed hollow.

"Yes, yes! Now we must help him to live again. First—on the cot there——"

Dard helped lift the man onto the cot in the middle of the room. Under direction he rubbed the icy flesh with oils from a bottle Kordov thrust upon him, watching the First Scientist inject various fluids over the heart and in scattered veins. Warmth was coming back into the body as they worked. And when the man had fully roused, been fed, and had fallen into the sudden second sleep, Dard aided in dressing him and helped transport the body up to the control cabin to be laid out on the accelerator mat.

"Who—oh, Cully!" Kimber identified the newly revived crewman. "That's good. Who else are you going to bring around?"

Kordov, puffing a little, took a moment to consider. "We have Santee, Rogan, and Macley there."

"The ship's not Santee's sort of job, and Cully's our

engineer. Wait a minute—Rogan! He's had space training—as a tel-visor expert. We'll need him——"

"Rogan it shall be then. But first we shall take a rest. We shall not need a tel-visor expert yet awhile, I believe?"

Kimber glanced at the timepiece set in the control board. "Not for about five hours at least. And maybe eight—if you want to be lazy."

"I am lazy when laziness is of advantage. Much of the troubles from which we have fled have been born of too much rushing about trying to keep busy. There is a time for working as hard as a man can work, yes. But there must also be hours to sit in the sun and think long thoughts and do nothing at all. Too much rushing wears out the body—and maybe also the mind. We must make haste slowly if we would make it at all!"

Whether it was some lingering effect of the cold sleep they could not decide, but they all found themselves dropping off into sudden naps. Kordov believed that the condition would pass, but Kimber was uneasy as they approached the chosen planet and demanded a stimulant from the First Scientist.

"I want to be awake now," Dard caught a scrap of conversation as he came back from a rest on one of the bunks in the other cabin. "To go off into a dream just when I take the ship into atmosphere—that's not possible. We aren't out of the woods yet—not by a long margin. Cully could take the controls in a pinch, so could Rogan, when you get him out of cold storage. But neither are trained pilots, and landing on unknown terrain is no job for a beginner!"

"Very well, Sim. You shall have your pill in plenty of time. But now you are to go in, lie down, and relax, not fight sleep. I promise that I shall rouse you in plenty of time. And meanwhile Cully will take your seat and watch the course——"

The tall thin engineer, who had said very little since his awakening, only nodded as he folded with loose-limbed ease into Kimber's reluctantly vacated place. He made some small adjustment on the control board and dropped his head back on the chair rest to watch the screen.

During the past hours the points of light had altered. The ball of flame Kimber designated as Sol II had slipped away over the edge of their narrow slice of vision. But the world they had chosen filled most of the expanse now, growing larger by seconds.

Kordov sat down in one of the other chairs to watch with Dard. The sphere on the screen now had a bluish-green tinge, with patches of other color.

"Polar regions—snow." Kordov commented.

Cully replied with a single, "Yeh!"

"And seas——"

To which Cully added the first long speech he had yet made.

"Got a lot of water. Should be picking up all land masses soon."

"Unless it's all water," mused Kordov. "Then," he grinned at Dard over his shoulder, "we shall be forced to leave it to the fish and try again."

"One thing missing," Cully adjusted the screen control for the second time. "No moon——"

No moon! Dard watched that enlarging sphere and for the first time since his awakening the dream-mood of passive acceptance of events cracked. To live under a sky where no silver globe ever hung. The moon gone! All the old songs men had sung, the old legends they had told and retold, the bit of history they cherished, that the moon was their first step into space, all gone. No moon—ever again!

"Then what will future poets find to rhyme with 'June' in all their effusions?" rumbled Kordov. "And our nights to come—they will be dark ones. But one can not have everything—even another stepping stone to space. That was how our moon served us—a way station, a beckoning sign post which lured us on and out. If there is or ever was intelligent life down there—they lacked that."

"No sign of space travel?" Cully wanted to know with a spark of interest.

"None. But of course, we can in no way be sure. Just because nothing has registered on our screens we can not say that it does not exist. If we were but a fraction off a well-traveled space lane we would not know it! And now, Dard, we have Rogan to rouse. I promised Sim that he would be on hand to share duty."

Again they made that trip below, lifted out the proper box and brought back to life the man who slumbered in it.

"That is the last one," stated Kordov when they had established Rogan in the control cabin. "No more until after we land. Hah!"

He had turned to look at the screen and the exclamation was jolted out of him by what he saw there. Land masses, mottled green-blue-red against which seas of a brighter hue washed.

"So we do not join fish. Instead you, Dard, must go and shake Sim back to life. Now is the time for him to be on duty!"

Shortly afterward Dard crouched on one of the acceleration mats beside the unconscious Rogan while the others occupied the chairs before the controls. The atmosphere within the cabin was tense and yet Kimber alone was at ease.

"Rogan come to yet?" he asked without turning his head.

Dard gently shook the shoulder of the man on the next mat. He stirred, muttered. Then his eyes opened and he scowled up at the roof of the cabin. A second later he sat up.

"We made it!" he shouted.

"That we did!" Kordov answered cheerfully. "And now—"

"Now there's a job waiting for you, fella," broke in Kimber. "Come up and tell us what you think of this."

Kordov spilled out of the third chair and helped Rogan into it. Holding tightly to the arms of the seat, as if he feared any moment to be tossed out of it, Rogan gave his full attention to the screen. He drew a deep breath of pure wonder.

"It's—it's beautiful!"

Dard agreed with that. The mingling of color was working on him—just as sunsets back on Terra had been able to do. There were no words he knew to describe what he now saw. But he didn't have a chance to watch long.

"Better strap down," came the suggestion from the pilot. "We're going in——"

Kordov plumped down on one of the acceleration mats, pulling the harness which flanked it up over his body, and Dard did the same. He was flat on his back against the spongy stuff of the pad with his head at an angle from which he could not see the screen. They bored into atmosphere and he must have blacked out, for he never afterward remembered the last part of the furious descent.

The ship shuddered, pushing up—or was it down—upon him. He had a misty idea that this must be full gravity returning. Then there was a shock which tore at the webs holding his body and he gasped, fighting for breath. But his hands were already at the buckles which fastened him down as he heard a voice say:

"End of the line! All out!"

And another replied—in Cully's dry tone: "Neat, Sim, nice and neat."

2. NEW WORLD

"ROGAN?"

The tel-visor expert had spun his seat around and was facing another section of the control panel, his fingers flying across the buttons there. Needles spun on dials, indicators moved, and Rogan's lips shaped words silently. When he had done Kimber flicked the control of the visa-screen which had gone dead at their landing.

Slowly pictures of the immediate surroundings of the ship unrolled before their fascinated eyes.

"Late afternoon," Rogan commented, "by the length of the shadows."

The ship had planted in the middle of an expanse of gray-blue gravel or sand—backed at a distance by perpendicular cliffs of reddish rock layered by strata of blue, yellow and white. As the scene changed, those in the control room saw the cliffs give way to the mouth of a long valley down the center of which curved a stream.

"That water's red!" Dard's surprise jolted the words out of him.

The red river was hemmed in by blue-green, low-growing vegetation which cloaked the ground within the valley itself and ran in tongues along the water into the semi-arid stretch of sand. Their viewing device was across the river, picking up more cliffs and sand. Then they were fronted by ocean shore and vivid aquamarine waves tipped with white lacy foam. Into this emptied the river, staining the sea red for some distance. Sea, air, cliffs, river—but no living creature!

"Wait!" Kimber's order sent Rogan's finger down on a button and the picture on the screen became fixed. "Thought I saw something—flying in the air. But guess I was wrong."

The scene changed until they were looking at the same spot where it had begun. Kimber stretched.

"This part of the country appears unoccupied. And, Tas, we didn't sight any signs of civilization when we came in either. Maybe our luck's held and we have an empty world."

"Hmm. But is it one we can venture into?" The First Scientist squeezed over to Cully's side of the cabin. "Atmosphere, temperature—within a fraction of Terra's. Yes, we can live and breathe here."

Kimber freed himself from the pilot's straps. "Suppose we have a look-see in person then."

Dard was the last to leave the cabin. He was still a little drunk with that riot of color on the visa-screen. After the remembered drabness of his home section of Terra this was overpowering. He was halfway down the ladder when he heard that clang which announced the opening of the hatch and the emergence of the ramp that would carry them safely over ground super-heated by their jets.

When he came out the others were strung along the ramp, breathing the warm air that was pungent with a fresh tang. The breeze pulled at Dard's hair, whipping a lock across his forehead, singing in his ears. Clean air—with none of the chemical taint which clung in the ship. Around the fins of their ship the sand had been fused into a curdled milky glass which they avoided by leaping from the end of the ramp to the dunes.

Kimber and Kordov plowed straight ahead to the wave-smoothed shore. Cully merely dropped in the soft grit of the beach, lying full length, his hands pressed tight to the earth, staring bemusedly up at the sky, while Rogan was pivoting slowly, as if to verify the scene the visa-screen had shown them.

Dard made his way to the sand. The redness of the river occupied him. Red water—why? The sea was normal enough except where it was colored by the river. He wanted to know what painted the stream and he started off determinedly to its bank.

The sand was softer, more powdery than any he had known on Terra. It shifted into his boot packs, arose in puffs and covered all but the faintest outline where he had stepped. He stooped and sifted the stuff through his fingers, knowing a strange tingle as the earth of this new world drifted away from his palm—blue sand—red river—red, yellow and white striped cliffs—color everywhere about him! Overhead that arch of cloud studded blue—or was it blue at all? Didn't it have just the faintest shading of green? Turquoise rather than true blue! Now that he was becoming accustomed to the color he could distinguish more subtle shades among the glows of brighter tones—shades he could not name—like that pale violet which streaked the sand.

Dard went on until he was in the stone-and-pebble-strewn border of the river. It was not a large stream, four strides might take him across it. There was a ripple of current but the water was opaque, dull rusty red, and it left a reddish rim about every stone it lipped in passage. He went down on one knee and was about to dip in a cautious exploratory finger when a voice called a warning:

"Don't try that, kid. Might not be healthy." Rogan came down the stony bank to join him. "Better be safe than sorry. Learned that myself on Venus—the hard way. See a piece of drift wood anywhere about?"

Dard searched among the rocks and found what appeared to be a very ordinary stick. But Rogan inspected it carefully before he picked it up. The stick was lowered into the flood and as cautiously withdrawn, an inch or so of it now dyed red. Together they held it close for examination.

"It's alive!" If he had been holding that test branch, Dard thought later, he might have dropped it at the realization of what the red stain was. But Rogan kept a tight grip.

"Lively little beggars, aren't they?" he asked. "Look like spiders. Do they float—or swim? And why so thick in the water. Now let's just see." He knelt and using the stick along the surface of the water skimmed off a good portion of what Dard secretly considered the extremely repulsive travelers. With the layer of "spiders" removed the water changed color becoming a clearer brownish fluid.

"So they can be scraped off," Rogan observed cheerfully. "With a strainer we may be able to get a drink—if this stuff is drinkable."

Dard swallowed hastily as Rogan tapped off on a convenient boulder the greater number of creatures he had fished out of the stream; and then together they followed the water to the sea. Several times they detoured, quite widely on Dard's part, to escape contact with patches of red marooned on shore. Not that the "spiders" appeared uncomfortable on the firmer element for they made no attempt to move away from the spots where some sudden eddy had deposited them.

A stiff breeze came in over the waves. It was heavy with the tang Rogan now identified for Dard.

"Natural sea—that's salt air!" What he might have added was drowned out by a hideous screech.

Close on its dying echo came a very human shout. Kimber and Kordov were running along the beach just beyond the water's edge. And above their heads twisted and darted a nightmare, a small nightmare to be sure, but still one horrible enough to have winged out of an evil dream.

If a Terran snake had been equipped with bat wings, two

clawed legs, a barbed tail, and a wide fanged mouth, it might have approached in general this horror. The whole thing could not have been more than eighteen or twenty inches long, but its snapping fury was several times larger than its body and it was making power dives at the running men.

Rogan dropped his spider stick as Dard's hand flew inside his blouse to claim the only possession he had brought from Terra. He threw a hunting knife and by some incredible luck clipped a wing, not only breaking the dragon's dive, but sending it fluttering down, end over end, screeching. It flapped and beat with the good wing, squirming across the sand until Kimber and Kordov pinned it to the shingle with hastily flung stones.

Its eyes gleamed with red hate as they gathered in a circle around it, avoiding the snapping jaws and the flipping of the barbed tail which now dripped oily yellow drops.

"Bet that's poison," suggested Rogan. "Nice critter—hope they don't grow any bigger."

"What's the matter?" Cully came tearing down the slope, one of the green ray guns in his hand. "What's making all that racket?"

Rogan moved aside to display the injured dragon. "Native-tive telling us off."

"Usually," Kimber broke in, "I don't believe in shooting first and investigating afterward. But this thing certainly hasn't any better nature to appeal to—nearly stripped he ear off my head before I knew he was around. Can you shoot it, Jorge, without messing it up too much? Tas, here, probably will want to take it apart later to see what makes it tick."

The biologist was squatting at a safe distance watching the convulsive struggles of the dragon with fascinated eyes. "Yes, please do not destroy it utterly. A snake—a flying snake! But that is not possible!"

"Maybe not on Terra," Kimber reminded him. "What can we say is possible or impossible here? Jorge, put it out of its misery!"

The green ray clipped the top of the creature's head and it went limp on the sand. Tas approached it gingerly, keeping as far as he could from the tail barb still exuding the yellow venom. Rogan went back down the beach to retrieve his spider collection, and Dard picked up and wiped his knife clean.

"Flying snakes and swimming spiders," the communications techneer held out his stick for their appraisal. "I'm going to be afraid to sit down out here—anything may pop up now."

Tas was plainly torn between the now tractable dragon and the water dwellers Rogan had brought him. "All this"— his pudgy hands indicated the world of cliffs, sand and sea —"new, unclassified."

Cully holstered his gun. He was frowning at the ceaseless waves.

"What do you make of those, Slim?" he demanded of the pilot, pointing to a low bank of clouds slowly expanding up the rim of the sky.

"On earth, I'd say a storm."

"Might be a bad one, too," Rogan commented. "And we have no shelter but the ship. At least this summer— we're warm enough."

"You think so?" asked Dard with some reason. The sea wind was rising, to become a wet lash with an icy bite in its flail. The temperature was dropping fast.

Kimber studied the clouds. "I'd say we better get back." But when he turned inland his gasp brought them all around.

They had left the star ship on an even keel. Now it listed so that its nose pointed down the valley away from the sea.

A good half hour later Kimber got to his feet, relief mirrored on his face. One of the fins had broken through the fused coating the jet heat had put on the beach. But beneath the splintered glass crust it had found rock support —it would slip no farther. The scarred sides towering above them were no longer mirror bright as they had been in the Cleft, she had too many years, too long a voyage behind her. But she was not going to fail them.

"Rock all right," Kimber repeated the statement he had made so joyfully a few minutes before. "The ledge slants a little, which is why she canted that way. But she'll stand. And," he did not need to draw their attention to the darkness closing in, "maybe it's some more luck at work again. With her nose pointing away from this breeze, she's less likely to come a cropper, even if it turns out to be a full-sized blow."

Dard held on to the rail of the ramp. The wind screamed around them, stirring up devils born of the powdery sand, which filled unwary eyes and any mouth that had the misfortune to be open. The dust had already driven Kordov inside, his precious dragon in a pair of forceps. He was more interested in that and Rogan's spiders than he now was in the ship.

"Full-sized blow?" drawled Rogan. "This has the makings of a hurricane if I'm any judge. And unless you fellas want to be buried alive in these marching sand dunes, you'd better run for cover. As long as you're sure we're not going to land bottom side up, I think it's time to adjourn."

Dard followed him up the ramp just in time to escape a miniature sandstorm through which the other two had to fight their way. There was a brushing-off party in the air lock, but, as they climbed back to the crew's quarters Dard could still taste grit in his mouth and hear it crunch under his feet.

Kordov was not to be found in the control cabin or bunk room when Kimber and the other two sat on the bunks and Dard dropped down cross-legged on the floor. The ship was vibrating under him. Could the wind have risen to that pitch already? It was Rogan who answered that.

"Like to see what's happening out there?" He got up and went into the control cabin.

Kimber and Dard got up to follow, but Cully shook his head.

"What you don't know, doesn't hurt you much," he remarked. "And I don't see anything exciting about a sandstorm."

It was true that when Rogan adjusted the visa-screen

there was little for them to see. The storm had brought night and obscurity. With an exclamation of annoyance, the techneer clicked off the viewer and they drifted back to find Cully asleep and Kordov climbing up to join them.

"Your 'spiders,' " he burst out as soon as he sighted Rogan, "are plants!"

"But they moved!" protested Dard. "They had legs."

Kordov shook his head. "Roots, not legs. And plants they are in spite of being mobile. Some form of aquatic fungi."

"Toadstools with legs yet!" Rogan laughed. "Next, trees with arms, I suppose. What about the dragon—was he a flying cabbage?"

Kordov did not need any urging to discuss the dragon. "Poisonous reptile—and carnivorous. We shall have to beware of them. But it was full grown, we need not worry."

"About their coming in larger sizes?" asked the relaxed Kimber in a lazy voice. "Let us be thankful for small favors and hope that they do a lot of screeching when they go ahunting. But now—let us think about tomorrow."

"And tomorrow—and tomorrow——" Rogan repeated sleepily but Cully sat up thoroughly aroused.

"When do we wake up the others?" he wanted to know. "And are we going to stay right here?"

Kordov locked his fingers behind his head and leaned back against the wall of the cabin. "I will revive Dr. Skort —Carlee—in the morning. She can help me with the others. Do you intend to explore the immediate terrain then? We should decide soon whether to stay here or try to find semi-permanent headquarters elsewhere."

"There is just one thing," said Kimber. "I can lift ship again, yes. But I can't guarantee another safe landing. The fuel—" he shrugged. "I don't know how long our voyage here lasted, but if we hadn't made this landfall when we did, we might not have been able to come in at all."

"So?" Kordov's lips shaped a soundless whistle. "Then we had better be very sure before we think of a move. What about taking out the 'sled'?"

"I'll break it out first thing tomorrow. That is, I will if this storm blows itself out by then. I don't propose to take that contraption up in a high wind—the bugs aren't out of it yet," Kimber retorted.

"And how about food?" Cully asked. "Specifically here and now for us, and objectively for the rest when they wake up."

"Specifically," Kordov opened one of the storage cabinets and took out five small packages which he tossed around to the company. "Concentrates. But, you're right, supplies are not going to last forever. We shall not be able to awaken all our company until we are reasonably sure of food and shelter. But—we'll get Harmon out of storage and have him investigate the soil up river where the vegetation is so thick. The exploration party might also hunt."

"Not dragons, I hope," Rogan mumbled through a mouthful of the dry concentrate cake. "I have a distinct feeling dragons will not agree with my internal arrangements! Or traveling fungi either——"

For the first time Dard ventured to break in upon his elders. "Some fungi—mushrooms—are good." He had no desire to lunch off red spiders, but he knew what real hunger meant and if it were a question of being hungry or eating swimming mushrooms, he could close his eyes and eat.

"Just so," Kordov beamed at him. "And we shall investigate the food value of these. I shall get the hamsters out of cold storage and try the local products on them."

"So if they don't curl up and go blue in the face we feast," Kimber stretched and yawned. "Since we have quite a full day before us tomorrow, suppose we hit the sack now. Toss for the bunks and the acceleration pads."

They solemnly tossed a coin—one with a hole in it which Kimber wore on a chain about his neck as a lucky piece. Dard found that Fortune relegated him to one of the acceleration pads and did not care. To his mind the soft sponge of that support was infinitely more comfortable than any bed he could remember.

But when he curled up on it he found that he could not sleep. All the wonders of the new world whirled through his mind in a mad dance. And behind him lurked fear. Lui

Skort had been a strong young man but he had not survived the passage. How many more of the boxes housed below in the star ship held death instead of life? What about Dessie?

Now that there was nothing to distract him, nothing he could give attention to, he remembered only her—the tight yellow braids sticking out at sharp angles, how she had been able to sit so quietly in the grass that birds and little animals accepted her as part of their world and had been entirely unafraid—how good and patient she had always been. Dessie!

He sat up. To lie there and sleep when Dessie might never wake to see this new land! He couldn't!

On his hands and knees Dard crawled out of the control cabin and between the bunks. Kimber was curled in a ball on one, but the other, which had fallen to Kordov, was empty. Dard started down the stair.

The deck below showed a patch of strong light and he could hear someone moving. He ventured to the door of the laboratory where he had helped to revive Cully and Rogan. The First Scientist was busy there, setting out instruments and bottles. He looked up as Dard's shadow fell into the room.

"What is it?"

"Dessie!" the boy blurted out. "I've got to know about Dessie!"

"Ah, so? But it is for their own comfort and protection that our companions must continue to sleep until we are sure of food and shelter."

"I know that." But the desperation in Dard could not be so sensibly silenced. "But—isn't there any way at all of telling? I have to know about Dessie—I just have to!"

Tas Kordov pulled out his lower lip with thumb and forefinger and allowed it to snap back into place with a soft smacking sound.

"That is a thought, my boy. We *can* tell whether the mechanism has in any way failed. And perhaps—just perhaps we can have other assurances. I must open that particular compartment in the morning anyway to bring out

Carlee Skort. Carlee—" his face puckered with the misery of an unhappy child. "And then I must be the one to tell her about Lui. That will be a very hard thing to do. Well, we do not escape the hard things in this life. Come along."

They went down five levels in the ship. Here the few lights were very dim, and the force of the wind against the hull could be more strongly felt. Kordov verified markings on the sealed door and at last released the fastening of a portal which came open with a faint sigh of displaced air. The chill of the room fed Dard's unease. He edged along after Kordov, between doubled racks of the coffin boxes to the final set. The First Scientist dropped to his knees and snapped on a hand torch to read dials.

"Dessie and Lara Skort are in this one together, they were so small they could share a compartment." The light in Kordov's hand flashed from one dial to the next, and the next. Then he smiled up at Dard.

"These are all as they should be, son. There has been no organic or chemical change inside since this was sealed. To my honest belief they are alive and well. Soon they will be out to run about as little girls should. They shall be free— as they never could have been on Terra. Do not worry. Your Dessie shall share this world with you!"

Dard had himself under control now and he was able to answer quite levelly:

"Thanks—thanks a lot, sir."

But Kordov had moved to another box and was reading more dials. He gave that case a slap of approbation as he straightened to his full height again.

"Carlee, too—we have been so very lucky."

3. STORM WRACK

"GOOD LORD!"

The tone rather than the words of that horrified exclamation awoke Dard and brought him up on the acceleration pad. Kimber, Rogan, and Cully were crowded together before the visa-screen. The hour might have been in the middle of the night, or late in the morning, for inside the ship day and night had no division. But on the screen it was day.

A gray sky was patched by ragged drifts of cloud. And as Dard leaned over the back of the pilot's seat, he saw what had so startled the others.

Where the day before there had stretched that smooth sweep of blue sand, forming a carpet clear to the base of the colorful cliffs, there was now only water, a sheet of it. Rogan set the viewer to turning so that they could see the flood completely surrounded the ship. Even the river had been swallowed up without any red stain left to betray its flow.

As the scene reached the seaside Rogan pushed the button which held it there. The beach was gone, it was the sea which had come in to enclose them.

"Surprise, surprise!" that was Rogan. "Do we now swim ashore?"

"I don't think that it is that deep," answered Kimber. "The water may come in this way during every hard storm. Switch over to the cliffs again, Les."

The picture whizzed with a dizzy speed back to the cliff. Kimber was right, already there was a stretch of sand showing at the base of that rock escarpment. The water was draining away.

They clattered down through the quiet ship, sending out

the ramp so that they could venture to the water's swirl. A weak current swilled around the fins and the bare sand at the cliff grew wider as they watched.

The flood was not clear, and caught around the fins of the ship were huge loops of weed. Some variety of fish had been beached close to the foot of the ramp, and a scaled tail beat waves as the stranded monster fought for life. Other debris showed tantalizingly now and again as the water was sullenly sucked away from the sand.

"What the——!" Cully's start was near to a jump. "Over —over to the right! What is that?"

Something *was* venturing out on the still-wet sand, following the retreating line of the sea. But, what it was, none of them dared guess. Kimber ran back into the ship while the rest tried vainly to see it better. The color was queer, a pale green, hardly to be distinguished from the sea water as it scurried along on four thin legs. But the outline of its head!

"Here!" Kimber skidded down the ramp, keeping himself out of the sea by a quick grab for the rail. He carried a pair of field glasses. "Is it still there—yes, I see it!" He focused the lenses in the right direction. "Great guns!"

"What is it?" demanded Rogan, plainly doing his best to keep from snatching the glasses away from the pilot.

"Yeah." Cully, too, was shaken out of his usual calm, "pass those along, fella! We all want a look-see!"

Dard squinted, trying to make natural sight serve as well as the lenses Kimber was now passing to Rogan. At least the thing on the sand did not appear to be alarmed either by the ship or the men watching it. Maybe it would stay in sight until he, as the very junior member of the party, had the right to use the lenses too.

It stayed, digging in the wet sand, until Cully did pass the glasses. Dard adjusted them feverishly. Having met the fungi spiders and a flying dragon, he could hardly be surprised by the weird beast he saw now. Its pale green skin was entirely hairless, nor was that skin scaled—instead it resembled to a marked degree his own smooth flesh. The creature's head was pear-shaped with ears which were hardly more than holes and large eyes set far apart so that the range of vision was probably wider than that of any Terran animal. But that pear head ended in what could only be described as a broad, duck's bill or hard blackish substance. And just as Dard trained the glasses upon it, it folded its hind legs neatly under it, to sit up in a doglike stance and gaze mildly across the dwindling tongue of sea straight at the star ship. Sand clung to its bill and it absent-mindedly brushed that off with a foreleg.

"Duck-dog." Kimber named it. "Doesn't look dangerous, does it? I'll be—! Just look at that!"

"That" was a short procession of more duck-dogs emerging from a dark crevice in the cliff to join the first. One of them, about three-quarters the size of the first, was the same pale green, but the three others were yellow, the exact yellow, Dard noted, of the strata in the cliff. In fact, as they marched by a projection of that particular stratum, they faded from sight. Two of the yellow beasts were full grown but the third was very small. And halfway along the path it sat down, refusing to move on until one of the larger animals returned to butt it ahead.

"Family party," suggested Dard, not daring to hold the glasses away from Kimber's impatient reach any longer.

"But harmless," the pilot suggested for the second time. "Do you suppose they'd let us near them? The water's gone down a lot."

"Nothing like trying. Just let Jorge be ready with that ray gun, then if they do turn out to be first-class menaces, we'll be prepared." The communications techneer lowered himself cautiously into the flood, which was at knee level.

He detoured to avoid the floating weed and paused when he reached the fish still beating the air with a frenzied tail. Dard caught up with him at that point.

Save for a curiously flattened head and a huge, paunchy middle, the stranded fish was the first living thing they had seen here which *did* resemble a Terran product. It was a good five feet long and displayed murderous teeth. The powerful tail beat the receding water into froth but it was beyond hope of escape. Dard spoke impulsively:

"Can't—can't you shoot it? It won't be able to get away and I think it knows that."

"Unhuh." That was Cully and as usual he wasted no words. He snapped the ray at that writhing head. With a last convulsion the fish flopped completely out of the water, to float with its huge belly up when it fell back.

"Maybe breakfast?" Rogan asked. "Looks a little bit like a tuna—might even taste like one. We'll let Kordov get it and see if it's fit for us to bury the teeth in. I could do with a steak—maybe two of them! Hello—the fireworks didn't send our duck-dogs running. I'd say they were enjoying the show."

Rogan was right. The duck-dog family party sat in a line along the crest of the fast drying sand ridge, appreciably closer to the ship, their attention all for the men and the now limp fish.

But as Dard tentatively splashed another step in the direction of that sand bank, the yellow members of the clan retreated, one of them nudging the smallest one in front of it. The green ones continued to stand their ground, the half-grown one running along the water's edge hissing. Dard stopped, the flood swishing about his legs.

Cully looped a cord about the tail of the dead fish and fastened it to the ramp rail. Perhaps overcome by the sight of so much meat, the smallest duck-dog gave a tiny whimpering cry and ran between the legs of its guardian to the water. Resignedly the larger yellow beast followed the cub, turning over the loose sand with large blunt claws of a forepaw to dig out a squirming red creature which the baby pounced upon to swallow greedily. But the green boss of the party hissed angrily at the hunter and sent both scuttling back.

Then he withdrew also, with his head turned toward the men, facing the danger represented by the Terrans bravely, hissing a stern warning. When the last of the smaller duck-dogs had dodged into the break in the cliff, he disappeared there also leaving only scuffed tracks in the sand to mark their trail. But Dard sighted the tip of a dark bill still protruding from the crack.

"It's still watching us."

"Wary," mused the pilot. "Which suggests that it has enemies—enemies which may look like us. But it's curious, too. If we ignore it—maybe——"

He was interrupted by a shout from the ship. Kordov had come out on the ramp and was waving vigorously to the explorers. As the others sloshed back he pulled on the cord, reeling in the fish.

"What's your verdict?" Rogan wanted to know when they joined him bending over their capture. "Do we eat that, or don't we?"

"Give me but a few minutes and some aid in the laboratory and I shall have an answer to that. But this is close to Terran life. So it may be edible. And what were you watching by the cliffs—more dragons?"

"Just passing the time of day with another breakfasting party," Rogan told him, and went on to explain about the duck-dogs.

It was worth waiting for Kordov's verdict, Dard thought later, as he savored the fine white flakes of meat, grilled under Kordov's supervision, and portioned out to the hungry and none-too-patient crew.

"At least we can chalk old pot-belly up on our bill of fare," observed Rogan.

"But finding this one may only be a fluke. It's a deepwater fish, and we won't have storms to drive such ashore every day," Kimber pointed out.

He explored his lips with his tongue and then studied the empty plastic plate he held wistfully. "We can, however, look around for another stranded one."

Cully unfolded long legs. "We'll take out the sled now?"

"The wind has died down—I'd say it was safe. And," the pilot turned to Kordov, "how about rousing Santee and Harmon—we're going to need them."

The First Scientist agreed. "But first Carlee, as a doctor. And then we shall bring out the others. You are leaving soon?"

"We'll tell you before we go. And we don't intend to go far. Maybe a turn into that valley up ahead, and then along the shore line for a mile or so. We may have landed in a wilderness—indications point to that—but I want to be sure."

Until a sun breaking through the clouds overhead said it was noon they were hard at work. The sled, Dard discovered, was just what its name implied, a flat vehicle possessing two seats each wide enough for two passengers, with a space behind for supplies. He helped to assemble the larger sections while Kimber and Cully sweated and swore over the business of installing the engine.

It was a flying craft Dard realized, but totally unlike a 'copter or rocket, and he did not see what would make it air borne without blades or tubes. When he said as much to Rogan the techneer leaned back against a convenient sand dune to combine rest and explanation.

"*I* can't tell you how it works, kid. The principle's something really new. They whipped that engine together during the last months we were in the Cleft. But it's some sort of anti-gravity. Takes you up and keeps you there until you shut it off. Broadcasts a beam which sends you along by pushing against the earth. If they had had the time they might have powered the ship with it. But there was only this one experimental sled built and we had to depend upon power we knew more about. How about it, Sim? Getting her together?"

The pilot smiled through a streak of grease which turned his brown skin black.

"Tighten that one bolt, Cully," he pointed out the necessary adjustment, "and, she's ready to lift! Or at least she should be. We'll try her."

He boarded the shallow craft and settled himself behind the controls, buckling a safety belt around his hips before he triggered the motor. The sled zoomed straight up with a speed which sent the spectators sprawling and tore an exclamation from the pilot. Then, under Kimber's expert hand, it leveled off and swung in a wide circle about the star ship. Finishing off the test flight with a figure eight, Kimber brought the sled back to a slow and studied landing on the now dry sand at the foot of the ramp.

"Bravo!"

That encouraging cheer came from the open hatch. Kordov beamed down at them and with him, one hand on the rail, her head lifted so that the sun made a red-glory of the braids wreathing it, was a woman. Dard stared up at her with no thought of rudeness. This was the Carlee who had taken care of Dessie.

But she was younger than he had expected, younger and somehow fragile. There were dark shadows beneath her eyes, and when she smiled at them, it was with a patient acceptance which hurt. Kimber broke the silence as she joined the party below.

"What do you think, Carlee?" he asked matter-of-factly, as if they had parted only the hour before and no tragedy lay between. "Would you trust yourself to this crazy flyer?"

"With the right pilot at the controls, yes." And then looking at each one she spoke their names slowly as if reassuring herself that they were really there. "Les Rogan, Jorge Cully and—" She reached Dard, hesitated, before her smile brightened—"why, you must be Dessie's Dard, Dard Nordis! Oh, this is good—so good——" She looked beyond the men at the cliffs, the sea, the blue-green sky arching over them.

"Now—before you start off, explorers," Kordov announced, "there is food to be eaten."

The food was fish again, together with quarter portions of the concentrate cakes and some capsules Kordov insisted they take. When they were finished the First Scientist turned to Kimber.

"Now that you have that sky-buggy of yours put together you will be off?"

"Yes. There are four, maybe five hours of daylight left. I think that a survey from the air would show us more in that length of time than a trip on foot."

"You say 'us.' Whom do you take with you?" asked Carlee.

"Rogan—he's had experience on Venus. And——"

Dard held his tongue. He could not beg to go. Kimber would choose Cully, of course. The pilot didn't want a green hand. He was so sure of that choice that he could hardly believe it when he heard Kimber say:

"And the kid—he's light weight. We don't want to overload if we haul back game or specimens, too. Cully's a crack shot and I'll feel safer to leave him on guard here."

"Good enough!" Kordov agreed. "Just do not voyage too far, and do not fall off that silly ship of yours—to land on your heads. We have no time to waste patching up explorers who do not know enough to keep themselves right side up!"

Thus Dard found himself sharing the pilot's seat on the sled with Rogan crawling in behind. Kimber insisted that they buckle their safety belts under his supervision and he tested their fastenings before they took off. The rise of the light craft was not so abrupt as the first time and Kimber did not try to get much above the level of the cliff tops. They skimmed along only a few feet above the rock as they flashed north, the curving shoreline as their guide.

From this height he had a good view to the west, seeing most of the wide valley through which the red river flowed. The low vegetation they sighted from the ship thickened into clumps of good-sized trees. And among these were flying things which did not appear to be dragons.

Along the edge of the sea the cliff rose in an unbroken perpendicular wall. Apparently the star ship had earthed in the only opening in it. For from the elevation of the sled they could sight nothing but that barrier of brilliantly hued stone dividing vegetation and low land from the beating sea.

Rogan cried out and a moment later Dard, too, cringed as a ray of light struck painfully into his eyes. It flashed up from sea level, as if a mirror had been used to direct the sunlight straight at them. Kimber brought the sled around and ventured out over the water in a sweep designed to bring them to the source of that light.

There was a scrap of beach, a few feet of sand across which the weed, driven up by the storm, lay. Kimber, with infinite caution, maneuvered to set them down there.

When the sled jolted to earth its occupants stared in open amazement at the source of the mirrored ray.

Protruding from the face of the cliff, as if from a pocket or hollow especially fashioned to contain it, was a cone-shaped section of metal. And not metal in a crude, unworked state, but of a finely fashioned and refined alloy!

Dard split a fingernail on the buckle which fastened his belt in his haste to get to the find. But Kimber was already halfway across the sand before he gained his feet. The three, not quite daring to touch, studied the peculiar object. Kimber squatted down to peer under it. There was a thin ring of similar metal encircling the widest part of the cone, as if it rested within a tube.

"A bullet in a rifle barrel!" Rogan found a comparison which was none too reassuring. "This a shell?"

"I don't think so." Kimber pulled gently at the tip. "Let's see if we can work it out." From the sled he brought an assortment of tools.

"Take it easy," Rogan eyed these preparations askance. "If it *is* an explosive, and we do the wrong thing—we're apt to finish up in pieces."

"It isn't a shell," Kimber repeated stubbornly. "And it's been here a long time. See that?" He pointed to fresh scars on the cliff face. "That's a recent break. Maybe the storm tore that down and uncovered this. Now—a little probing."

They worked gingerly at first, and then, when nothing happened, with more confidence—until they had it out far enough to see that the cone was only the tip of a long cylinder. Finally they hooked a chain to it and used the power of the sled to draw it completely free of the tube.

Six feet long, it lay half in, half out of the water, a sealed opening showing midway in its length. Kimber knelt down before the tube and flashed his hand-light inside. As far as they could see ran a tunnel lined with seamless metal.

"What in the name of Space is it, anyway?" Rogan wondered.

"Some form of transportation, I would say." Kimber still

THE STARS ARE OURS

held the light inside as if by wishing alone he could de-
duce the destination of their discovery.

Rogan prodded the cylinder with his foot and it rolled
slightly. The techneer stooped and tugged at the end in
the sand. To his astonishment he was able to lift it several
inches above the beach.

"A whole lot lighter than you'd think! I believe we could
take it back on the sled!"

"Hmm . . ." Kimber took Rogan's place and hoisted.
"We might at that. No harm in trying."

The three of them manhandled the cylinder on board the
sled and lashed it into place—though both ends projected
over the sides of the craft.

Kimber was doubly careful in his take-off. He brought
them up with much room to spare away from the cliff side
and circled back toward the valley.

"This answers one question," Rogan leaned forward.
"We aren't the first intelligent life here."

"Yes." The pilot added nothing to that bare assent. He
was intent on reaching the star ship.

Dard squirmed in his seat. He did not need to turn to
see that smooth piece of metal, he could feel its presence—
and what its presence meant to all of them.

Only intelligence, a high standard of intelligence could
have fashioned it. And where was that intelligent life now?
Watching and waiting for the Terrans to make the first
fatal move?

4. THOSE OTHERS!

"EASY DOES IT NOW." Cully laid down the chisel he had
been using delicately and applied pressure with the flat of
his hand.

The others weren't really breathing down his neck.
But they did struggle against the curiosity which made

them crowd about the engineer as he worked to open the cylinder.

"It's too light for an explosive," Rogan repeated for about the fiftieth time since they had unloaded their find before the star ship.

At a good vantage point up on the ramp Carlee Skort and Trude Harmon sat together while the men below tried to hand Cully tools he didn't need and generally got in each other's way. But now they had come to the last moment of suspense. After more than an hour's work the engineer had been able to force open the small seal hatch.

Cully bumped heads with Kimber and Kordov as he flashed a torch beam into the interior. Then, with infinite care, he began to hand out to eager assistants a series of boxes, small round containers and a larger, ornamented chest. All these were fashioned of the same lightweight alloy as the large carrier and they appeared unmarked by time.

"Cargo carrier," Kimber decided. "What can be in these?" He held one of the smallest boxes to his ear and shook it cautiously, but there was no answering rattle.

Kordov picked up the chest, examining its fastening carefully. At last he shook his head and brought out a pocket knife, working the blade into the crevice between lid and side, using it to lever up the cover.

Soft creamy stuff puffed up as the pressure of the lid was removed, fluffing over the rim. The First Scientist plucked it carefully away in strips. As the late afternoon sun struck full on the contents which had been protected by that packing, there was a concerted gasp from the Terrans.

"What *are* they?" someone demanded.

Kordov picked up a fine intwisted strand, dangling its length in the light.

"Opals?" he suggested. "No, these are too hard, cut in facets. Diamonds—? I don't think so. I confess I have never seen anything like them before."

"A world's ransom," Dard did not know he had spoken

aloud. The wild beauty swinging from Kordov's hand drew him as no man-fashioned thing had done before.

"Any more in there?" asked Kimber. "That's a large box to hold only one item."

"We shall see. Girls," Kordov held out the rope of strange jewels to the two women, "hang on to that."

Another layer of the packing was pulled out to display a pair of bracelets. This time red stones which Santee identified.

"Them's rubies! I prospected in the Lunar mountains and found some just like 'em. Good color. What else you got there, Tas?"

A third layer of packing led to the last and greatest wonder of all—a belt, five inches wide, with a clasp so set in gems as to be just an oval glitter—the belt itself fashioned of rows of tiny crystalline chains.

Trude Harmon tried to clasp it about her waist to discover it would not meet by inches. Nor was Carlee able to wear it either.

"Must have been mighty slim, the girl what wore that!" Harmon commented.

"Maybe she wasn't a girl at all," Carlee said.

And there was something daunting in that thought. Carlee had been the first to put into words their lurking fear, that those who had packed the carrier had been nonhuman.

"Well, bracelets argue arms," Rogan pointed out. "And that necklace went around a neck. A belt suggests a waist—even if it is smaller than yours, girls. I think we can believe that the lady those were meant for wasn't too far removed from our norm."

Santee pawed another box away from the pile. "Let's see the rest."

The boxes were sealed with a strip of softer metal which had to be peeled from around the edge. And the first three they forced contained unidentifiable contents. Two held packages of dried twigs and leaves, the third vials filled with various powders and a dark scum which might have been the remains of liquid. These were turned over to Kordov for further investigation.

Of the remaining boxes three were larger and heavier. Dard broke the end of the sealing strip on one and rolled it away. Under the lid was a square of coarse woven stuff folded over several times to serve as protective padding. Since this was like the jewel case the others stopped their own delving and gathered around as he pulled the stuff loose. What he found beneath was almost as precious in its way as the gems.

He dared not put his fingers on it, but worked it out of the container gently by the end of the metal rod on which it was wound in a bolt. For here was a length of fabric. But none of them—not even those who could remember the wonders of the pre-Burn cities—had ever seen anything such as this. It was opalescent, fiery color rippled along every crease and fold as Dard turned it around in the sunlight. It might have been spun from the substance of those same jewels which formed the necklace.

Carlee almost snatched it from him and Trude Harmon inserted a timid finger under the edge.

"It's a veil!" she cried. "How wonderful!"

"Open the rest of those!" Carlee pointed to the two similar boxes. "Maybe there's more of this."

There was more fabric, not so sheer and not opalescent, but woven of changing colors in delicate subtle shades the Terrans could not put names to. Inspired by this find they plunged into a frenzy of opening until Kordov called them to order.

"These," he indicated the wealth from the plundered boxes, "can't be anything but luxury goods, luxury goods of a civilization far more advanced than ours. I'm inclined to believe that this was a shipment which never reached its destination."

"That tube we found the carrier in," mused Kimber. "Suppose they shot such containers through tubes for long distances. Even across the sea. We didn't transport goods that way, but we can't judge this world by Terra. And they have no high tides here."

"Tas, Sim," Carlee turned one of the bracelets around in hands which bore the scars of the hardworking Cleft life, "could they—are they still here? Those Others—?"

Kimber got to his feet, brushing the sand from his breeches.

"That's what we'll have to find out—and soon!" He squinted at the sun. "Too late to do anything more today. But tomorrow—"

"Hey!" Rogan balanced on his palm a tiny roll of black stuff he had just pried out of a pencil-slim container. "I think that this is some kind of microfilm. Maybe we can check on that—if we can rig up a viewer which will take it."

Kordov was instantly alert. "How many of those things in there?"

Rogan took them one at a time from the box he had opened. "I see twenty."

"Can you rig a viewer?" was Kordov's next question.

The techneer shrugged. "I can try. But I'll have to get at machines we packed in the bottom storeroom—and that will take some doing."

"And"—Cully had been poking in the interior of the now empty carrier—"there's an engine in here—must have supplied the motive power. I'd like to dig it out and see what makes it tick."

Kimber ran his hands over the tight cap of his hair. "And you'll need a machine shop to do that in, I suppose?" He was very close to sarcasm. "There's the problem of those still in the ship—what will we do?"

Carlee broke in. "You haven't found any signs of civilization yet—except this. And you don't know how long this could have lain where you discovered it. We can't hold off settlement until we are sure. The cities, or centers of civilization—if there are any—may be hundreds of miles away. Suppose a space ship had landed on Terra in a center section of the Canadian northwest, on the steppes of Central Asia, or in the middle of Australia—any thinly populated district. It would have been months, perhaps years, before its arrival became known—especially since Pax forbade travel. There may exist a similar situation here. Our landing may go undiscovered for a long time—if we do share this world."

"And that, you know," Kordov added, "is common sense. Let us explore the valley—if it is promising, make a place there for our people. But at the same time an exploring team can operate to map the district. Only, let us not make contact with any race we find, until we know its attitude."

"Or what manner of creature," Carlee said softly to herself.

What manner of creature. Dard had caught that. Carlee most likely believed that the intelligence which might share this world was nonhuman. Man's old fear of the unknown, the not-understood, would again haunt them. This was an alien world, could they ever make it home?

"These—these are beautiful!" Trude Harmon had knelt beside him in the sand to see the small carvings he was mechanically unwrapping.

The one he held represented an animal which was a weird cross between horse and deer—possessing flowing mane, tail and horns. Presented as rearing, with snorting nostrils, it was a miniature of savage fury. Tiny gems were set in the eye sockets and the hooves were plated with a contrasting metal. Some master-craftsman had endowed it with life.

"All these things—they are so wonderful!"

"They loved beauty," Dard answered her. "But I think that these"—he picked up a second carving, representing quite a different creature—a manikin with webbed feet, a monkey face and hands lacking a thumb—"are all pieces to be used in a game. See, here's another horned horse, but made of a different color, and another webfooted monkey. Chessmen?"

"And a little tree!" She freed a third piece from its wrappings. "A tree of golden apples!"

True enough, on the branches of the cone shaped tree there were round gems of a glowing yellow. Golden apples! That story Lars used to tell Dessie about the apples of the sun!

131

"Huh?" Harmon squatted down by his wife to see what held her attention. "Apples? What's that about apples, Trude?"

She held out her hand with the small tree standing on its flattened palm. "Golden apples! See, Tim?"

"Looks more like some kind of a pine to me." But he took the tree gently. "Fruit—that's what those are supposed to be all right." His eyes went past the star ship to the open mouth of the valley where the blue-green of growing things beckoned. "Might find us a pine growin' apples at that, Trude. After them there flyin' snakes, and floatin' spider-plants, and them green and yellow duck-dogs what keep peekin' at us from holes yonder—well, I can believe that we're gonna pick us apples offa pine trees, too. Only we'd better get about the business of goin' to hunt them trees pretty soon."

The business of hunting their future settlement began the next morning. Kimber with Rogan and Santee took off in the sled to make a circuit of the inner valley. When they signaled that they viewed nothing disturbing there, a second exploring party set off on foot. Cully, Harmon and Dard, with packets of supplies, stun rifles and water-filled canteens progressed slowly up the river.

At the entrance to the inner valley the sand was broken by patches of soil shading from red-yellow to a dark brown. In this earth grew tufts and clumps of thin-bladed, very tough-stemmed grass which in its turn gave way to small bushes, clothed with ragged blue-green leaves.

All three of the explorers stopped short as the grass before them swayed, masking the progress of some living thing. Dard was the first to move forward with his silent woodsman's tread. Cautiously he parted the tall stalks to see below him a real path, as well marked as a Terran game trail, but in miniature. As the swaying still continued he stood waiting, hardly daring to breath.

Around the roots of a low bush a small red-brown head, almost indistinguishable from the bare earth of the trail, showed. Dard waited. With a hop the traveler came into plain sight.

Close to the size of a Terran rat it hopped on large, overdeveloped hind legs, between which bobbed a fluff of tail. Small handlike paws hung down across its darker belly fur. The ears were large, fan shaped, and fringed with the same fluff as the tail. Black buttons of eyes showed neither pupil nor iris, and a rounded muzzle ended in a rodent's prominent teeth. But Dard did not have long to catalogue such physical points. It sighted him. Then it gave a wild bound, making an about-face turn while in the air—disappearing in a second. Dard was left to pick up from the center of the trail the object it had just dropped in its flight.

"Rabbit?" Harmon wondered, "or squirrel or rat? How're we gonna know? What did that critter drop, boy?"

Dard held a pod about three inches long, dark blue and shiny. He surrendered it to Harmon who slit the outer covering with thumbnail and shook out a dozen dark-blue seeds.

"Pears, beans, wheat?" Harmon's bewilderment showed signs of irritation. "It grows, ripens this way, and it may be good to eat. But," he turned to his companions and ended with an explosive, "how're we gonna know?"

"Take 'em back and try 'em on the hamsters," Cully returned laconically. "But that hopper sure could go, couldn't he?" Thus he unconsciously christened the third type of fauna they had discovered in the new world.

Harmon stowed seeds and pod away in a zipper closed pocket, before they moved on through grass which arose waist high about them. Here and there in it they spotted more of the seed pods.

In fact shortly the pod-headed plants were so thick around them that they might have been swishing through a field of ripened grain. Harmon broke silence:

"This remind you of anything?"

They regarded the expanse of blue doubtfully and shook their heads.

"Well, it does me. This here looks jus' like a wheatfield all ready t' be reaped! I tell you I'm athinkin' we're walkin' over somebody's farm!"

"But there's no fences," protested Dard.

"No, but you take a farm that's not been touched for a good long time—this stuff coulda jus' kept seedin' itself and spread out a lot. I gotta feelin' this is part of a farm."

With that Harmon took the lead, cutting across the narrowest section of the ripe crop to a line of bushes. Now that his attention had been stimulated by Harmon's theory Dard thought that that clump of taller vegetation was strung out as if it might provide a barrier for the grain, a fence for the field.

They worked their way around this line of brush to discover Harmon's instinct right. For there was no disguising the artificiality of the large dome flanked by several smaller ones which stood surmounted and surrounded by rank vines, tall grass and long unpruned shrubbery.

But it was not those domes which held the explorers' attention. A constant murmur of sound and a flash of flying things drew them to a tree standing in what once must have been the front yard—if Those Others cultivated front yards.

"The golden apples!" Dard identified the tree from the carved piece he had seen the night before.

Its symmetrical cone shape of blue-green provided the right background for the yellow globes which dragged down branches with their weight. And the air and grass about the tree were alive with feasters.

The Terrans watched the wheeling birds—or were they oversized butterflies—that settled and squabbled for a chance to sink beaks into those ripened orbs. While, on the ground, there was a steady coming and going of hoppers harvesting the soft fallen fruit. And from that scene of activity the breeze wafted a scent which set the watchers' mouths watering—semi-intoxicating with its promise of juicy delights.

As the men advanced, the busy feeders displayed no signs of alarm. One hopper ran straight between Cully's feet, a quarter section of dripping fruit clasped in its arms. And a bird-butterfly skimmed Dard's head on its way to the banquet.

"Well—for—!" Cully caught himself in midstride to avoid

stepping on a furry red-brown mass. He picked up one of the hoppers in a completely comatose state. Harmon gave a bark of laughter.

"Dead drunk," he commented. "Seen chickens—pigs, too—get that way on cider leavin's. Lookit here—this bird can't fly straight neither!"

He was right. A lavender creature, whose wings were banded with pale green and gray, flapped an erratic course to a nearby bush and clung there as if it did not trust its powers for a farther flight.

Cully laid down the limp hopper and picked one of the golden apples. It snapped away easily, and he held it out for their closer examination. The skin was firm over the pulp, and radiating out from the stem were tiny rosy freckles. And the enticing scent was a temptation hard to withstand. Dard wanted to snatch the fruit from the engineer, to sink his teeth in that smooth skin and prove to himself that it tasted as good as it smelled.

"Pity we ain't got a hamster with us to try it on. But we can take some back. Iffen they're good," Harmon swallowed visibly, "we can have us some real eatin'! Needn't let the critters take 'em all. The fella what lived here, I bet he set a store by them there things. Golden apples, yeah, that's jus' what they be. But they ain't gonna run away, and me, I'd kinda like to see the house and barns."

The house and barns, if those were the correct designations for the domes, were half buried in twisting vines and rank growth. When they broke their way through to what must have been the front door of the largest dome, Cully let out his breath in a low whistle.

"Fight here. This door was smashed in from the outside."

Dard, accustomed to the violence of the raiding parties of Pax, noted the broken scraps of metal on the portal and agreed. They edged into a scene of desolation. The place had been looted long ago, tough grass grew through a crack in the wall, and the litter underfoot went to powder when their boots touched it. Dard picked up a shred of golden glass which held a fairy tracery of white pattern. But there was nothing whole left.

"Raiding party, all right," Harmon agreed, conditioned by his Terran past. "Could be that they had them some Peacemen here too. But it was a long time ago. We'd better let Kordov and the brains prospect around in here. Maybe they can learn what really happened. Wonder if the barn took a beatin'."

But what they did discover in the larger of the two remaining domes brought a steady stream of curses from Harmon and made Dard's skin crawl with its suggestion of wanton and horrible rapine. A line of white skeletons lay along the wall, each in what seemed a stall. Harmon tried to pick up an oddly shaped skull which went to dust in his fingers.

"Left 'em to die of thirst and starvation!" gritted the farmer. "Knocked off the people and jus' left the rest. They—they were worse'n Peacemen—them what did this!"

"And they must have been the winners, too," observed Cully. "Not too pleasant to think about."

All three started at a shout, and Dard swung his stun rifle around at the entrance of that tragic barn. What if "they" were returning? Then he forced imagination under control. This horror had occurred years ago—its perpetrators were long since dead. But had they left descendants— with the same characteristics?

Kimber came into the dome. "What're you doing in here?" he wanted to know. "We've been watching you from the sled. What—what in blue blazes is this?"

"Warning left by some very nasty people," Dard spoke up. "This farm was raided and whoever did it left the animals penned up to starve to death!"

Kimber walked slowly along that pitiful line of bones. His face was very sober indeed.

"It's been a long time since this happened." It appeared to Dard that the pilot was reassuring himself by that statement.

"Yeah," Harmon agreed. "A good long time. And they

ain't bin back since. Guess we can move down here and take over, Sim. This was a good farm once, no reason why it can't be one agin."

5. WAR RUIN

FOR THE NEXT five days they were well occupied. An extensive exploration of the inner valley, on foot and in the air, revealed no other evidences of the former civilization. And the Terrans decided against inhabiting the farm. About those domes there clung the shreds of ancient fear and disaster, and Dard was not the only one to feel uneasy within their walls.

The tree of golden apples was one of their best finds. The hamsters relished the fruit and, so encouraged, the humans raided along with the valley's furred and feathered inhabitants, because the globes were as good as they looked and smelled—though their intoxicating effect did not hold with the Terrans. The grain also proved to be useful, and Harmon took the risk of rousing one of the two heifer calves, carried in the ship, and feeding it in the forsaken fields where it lived and grew fat.

On the other hand a bright green berry with a purplish blush was almost fatal to a hamster and had to be shunned by the Terrans, although the hoppers and the birds gorged upon it.

Quarters were established, not outside the cliffs which walled the valley, but within them. The second day's exploration had located a cave which led in turn to an inner system of galleries, through one of which the rivers wove a way. Habituated to such a dwelling from their years in the Cleft, they seized upon this discovery eagerly. More of the adult passengers were awakened and put to work assembling machines, laboring to make the caves into a new home which could not be easily detected. For the threat kept before them by the ruined farm was always in their minds.

Three more bodies were carried from the star ship to be interred beside Lui Skort, still encased in the boxes which had held them during the voyage. But Kordov continued to insist that they had been very lucky. There were fifteen men at work now, and ten women added their strength to harvesting the strange grain and making habitable the cave dwelling.

"Blast it!" Kimber drew out of the motor section of the sled and made a grab at thin air.

"What's the matter?" Dard began. Then he caught sight of what had brought the pilot to the exploding point.

A hopper bounded toward the tall grass, something shiny between its front paws. Stealing again!

Dard dived, and his fingers closed about the small, frantically kicking body, while a squeak which approached a scream rent the quiet of their outdoor workshop. The boy freed his captive to nurse a bitten hand, but the hopper had also dropped the bolt it had stolen. Now it retired empty pawed into the bushes uttering impolite remarks concerning Dard's destination and ancestry.

"Better go and have that bite looked after," Kimber ordered with resignation as he accepted the rescued bolt. "I don't know what we are going to do about those little beasts. They'd carry off everything they could lug if we didn't watch them all the time. Regular pack rats."

Dard cradled the bitten hand in the other. "I'd like to find one of their burrows, or nests, or whatever they build to keep their loot in. It should be a regular curiosity shop."

"If any one can—you will," Cully spoke from the cylinder he was dismantling. "Ever notice, Sim," he continued, "how this kid gets around? I'll wager he could walk through the grain field and not make a sound or leave a trail another could follow. How'd you ever learn that useful trick, fella?"

Dard was sober. "The hard way, living as an outlaw. You know, those hoppers *are* awful pests, but I can't help admiring them."

Kimber snorted. "Why? Because they know what they want and go after it? They are single-minded aren't they?

Only I wish they were a little more timid. They should be more like the duck-dogs, willing to watch us, but keeping their distance. Cut along, kid, and get that finger seen to right away. Working hours aren't over yet."

Dard traced Carlee Skort to where she was busy fitting up the small dispensary, a niche in the wall of the second cave, and had his bite sterilized and bandaged with plasta-skin.

"Hoppers!" She shook her head. "I don't know what we're going to do to discourage them. They stole Trude's little paring knife yesterday and three spools of thread."

He could understand her dismay over these losses. Little things, yes—but articles which could not be replaced.

"Luckily they appear to be afraid to come into the caves. So far we haven't caught any of them inside. But they are the most persistent and accomplished thieves I have ever seen. Dard, when you go out, stop in the kitchen and pick up a lunch for your working crew. Trude should have the packets made up by now."

He obediently made his way past work gangs into the other small cave room where Trude Harmon with an assistant was setting out stacks of plastic containers. The rich scent which filled the air tickled Dard's nose and made him very aware of hunger. It had been hours and hours since breakfast!

"Oh, it's you," Trude greeted him. "How many in your gang?"

"Three."

Her lips moved, counting silently, as she apportioned the containers and set them in a carrier.

"Mind you bring those back. And don't, don't you dare leave them where any hoppers can put paw on them!"

"No, ma'am. Something sure smells good."

She smiled proudly. "Those golden apples. We stewed some up into a kind of pudding. Just you wait 'til you taste it, young man. Which reminds me—where is that queer leaf, Petra?"

The dark-haired girl who had been stirring the largest pot on the stove pulled a glossy green leaf from one of her pockets. It was an almost perfect triangle in shape—green, threaded by bright red and yellow veins.

"Ever see one like that before, Dard?" Trude asked.

He took it and examined it curiously before he answered with a shake of his head.

"Pinch it and give a sniff!" Trude suggested.

He did and the good odor of cooking was nullified by another aromatic, clean fragrance, a mixture of herb and flower—of all the pleasant scents he had ever known.

"You can rub it on skin or hair and the scent lingers," Petra told him eagerly.

"And you'll never guess where we got that one," Trude broke in. "Tell him."

"I saw a hopper carrying it out in the grain field when I was gleaning yesterday. I thought it had been stealing from our food and chased it. Then when it wriggled through a hole in the brush fence it dropped the leaf. I picked it up and at first we thought it might be good to eat because the hopper wanted it. But it is just nice perfume."

"Sure, and if you want to get on the good side of the kitchen detail," Trude twinkled at him, "you just find out where you can get about a peck of those, Dard. We ain't got the smell of that ship off us yet—nasty chemicals. And we'd admire a chance to get some perfume. You do a little looking around when you're off on this jaunt of yours and see what you can find us. Now—clear out. Take your lunch."

Dard gave the leaf back to Petra and picked up the carrier. But he went out of the kitchen puzzled. What had Trude meant by "this jaunt of yours?" As far as he knew he was not intending to leave the valley. Had some other plans been made?

He started back to Kimber, determined to have an explanation.

"Lunch, huh?" Cully crawled out from under the cylinder as Dard sat the carrier on the ground.

The engineer wiped his hands on the grass and then on a piece of waste. "What do they have for us this time?"

"Stew of apples for one thing," Dard returned impatiently. "Listen, Kimber, Mrs. Harmon said something about my going on an expedition."

Sim Kimber pried the lid off a container of stew and poked into the depths of the savory mixture before he replied.

"We have to earn our keep, kid. And not being specialists in anything but woodcraft and transportation, it's up to us to do what we can along those lines. You knew the woods and mountains back on earth, and you have a feeling for animals. So Kordov assigned you to the exploration department."

Dard sat very still, afraid to answer, afraid to burst out with the wild exultation which surged in him now. He had tried, tried so hard these past few days to follow Harmon's overpowering interest in the land, to be another, if unskilled, pair of hands in the work about the cave. But the machines they were assembling at top speed were totally unknown to him. The men who worked on them lapsed into a jargon of functions he knew nothing about, until it seemed that they jabbered a foreign tongue.

For so long he had been responsible for others—for Lars and Dessie, for their food, their shelter, even their safety. And now he was not even responsible for himself. He was beginning to feel useless, for here he knew so little that was of any account.

All his training had been slanted toward keeping alive, at a minimum level of existence, in a hostile world. With that pressure removed he believed he had nothing to offer the colonists.

What he had dreamed and longed to do was to leave this compact group where he was the outsider, to go on into this new world, searching out its wonders, whether that meant trailing a hopper to its mysterious lair or flying above the cliffs into the unknown country beyond. Exploration was what he wanted, wanted so badly that sometimes just thinking about it hurt.

And here was Kimber offering him that very thing! Dard could not say anything. But maybe his eyes, his rapturous face answered for him, as the pilot glanced up, met Dard's wide happy eyes, and quickly looked away. When the boy's feelings were under control again, and he was able to say, in what he believed was a level and unmoved voice:

"But what are you planning?"

"Go up and over." It was Cully who answered that before Kimber could swallow his mouthful of stew. "We load up this old bus," the engineer patted the sled affectionately, "and take off to see what lies on the other side of the cliffs. Mainly to discover whether we need expect any visitors."

"We—who?"

Kimber named those who would share in the adventure.

"I'll pilot. Cully goes along to keep the sled ticking. And Santee is to provide the strong right arm."

"To fight—?" But Dard didn't complete that question before Kimber had an answer.

"Killing," he said, staring thoughtfully down at the full spoon he balanced on its way to his mouth, "is not on the program if we can help it. Even such pests as—Cully! behind you!"

The engineer slowed around just in time to snatch up a small wrench and so baffle the furry thief that tried to seize it.

"Even those pests are safe from us," Kimber continued before he added to the swearing engineer, "Why don't you sit on everything, Jorge? That's what I am doing." He moved to let them see that all the smaller tools he had been using were now covered by his body. "It may not be comfortable, but they'll still be here when I need them!

"No," he returned to his earlier theme, "we're not going to kill anything if we can help it. To save our lives—for food, if it is absolutely necessary. But not for sport—or because we are unsure!" His lips twisted in a sneer. "Sport! The greatest sport of all is the hunting of man! As man finally discovered, having terrorized all of the rest of the living earth. Our species killed wantonly—now we have a second choice and chance. Maybe we can be saner this time. So—Santee is a crack shot—but that does not mean he is going to use the rifle."

Dard had only one more question. "When do we go?"

"Tomorrow morning, early. On our last swing around the cliffs two days ago we sighted indications of a road leading eastward from the other side. It could be the guide we want."

They finished their work upon the sled in mid-afternoon and the remaining hours of work time stowing away supplies and equipment. Kimber made preparations for five days' absence from the valley—flying east to the interior of the land mass on which the star ship had earthed.

"That tube we found pointed in that direction. If it was a freight carrier for some city—and I am of the opinion that it was—that's where we may find the remains of civilization." Kimber's voice came muffled as he checked dials behind the wind screen of the aircraft.

"Yeah." Santee added a small bag of his own to the supplies. "But—after what we seen at that there farmhouse —they played rough around here once upon a time. Better watch out that we don't get shot down before we make peace signs."

"It's been a long time since the farm was looted," Dard ventured to point out. "And why didn't the looters return —if they were the winners in some war. Harmon says this land is rich, that any farmer would settle here."

"Soldiers ain't farmers," said Santee. "Me, I'd say this was lootin' done by an army or somebody like them blasted Peacemen. They was out to smash and grab and run. Land don't mean nothin', to them kinda guys. But I see what Harmon means. If the war ended why didn't somebody come back here to rebuild? Yeah, that's sense."

"Maybe there was no one left," Dard said.

"Blew themselves up?" Kimber's expressive eyebrows rose as he considered that. "Kind of wholesale, even for a big-time war. The burn-off took most of Terra's cities and the purge killed off the people who could rebuild them. But there were still plenty of men kicking around afterward. Of course, they were ahead of us technically here— those things in the carrier point to that. Which argues that—if they were like us—they were way ahead in the production of bigger and more lethal weapons, too. Well, I have a feeling that tomorrow or the next day we're going to learn about it."

The light was that gray wash which preceded sunrise when Dard sat up in his bedroll to answer the shadowy figure who roused him. He shivered, more with excitement than the morning chill, as he rolled his bag together and stole after Cully out of the cave to the sled.

There the four explorers made a hasty breakfast on cold scraps while Kimber talked disjointedly with Kordov, Harmond and Rogan.

"We'll say five days," he said. "But it may be longer. Give us a good margin for error. And don't send out after us if we don't make it back. Just take precautions."

Kordov shook his head. "No man is expendable here, Sim, not any more. But why should we borrow trouble in such large handfuls? I will not believe that you won't return! You have the list of plants, of things you are to look for?"

Simba Kimber touched a breast pocket in answer. Cully took his place in the second seat of the sled and beckoned Dard to join him. When Kimber was behind the control Santee scrambled in, a stun rifle across his big knees.

"I'll listen for any broadcast," Rogan promised. And Harmond mouthed something which might have been either reminder or farewell as Kimber took them up into the crisp air of the dawn.

Dard was too excited to waste any time waving goodbye or looking back into the safety of the valley. Instead he was leaning forward, his body tense, as if by the sheer power of his will he could speed their flight into the unknown.

They kept to a speed about equal to that of a running man as they followed the cliffs along to the narrow upper end of the valley. Close packed below to the edge of those stone walls was the woods the exploring parties had located earlier, only to be kept from penetration by the density of the growth.

"Queer stuff," Cully remarked now as they soared over

the tree tops. "A limb grows long, bends over to the ground, touches, then takes root and another tree starts to grow out right there. That whole mass down there may have started with just one tree. And you can't break or hack through it!"

The sky before them was bannered with pink streamers. A flight of the delicately hued butterfly-birds circled them and then flew as escort until they were just beyond the valley wall. What the explorers saw beneath them now was a somber earth-covering blanket of blue-green, vaguely dismal and depressing with its unchanging darkness. Another collection of the self-planting trees made an effective barrier along the eastern side of the cliffs, and this was not a small wood but a far-stretching forest.

"There!" Santee pointed downward. "That there's it! Them trees cover it some, but I say it's a road!"

A narrow ribbon of a light-colored substance, hidden for long distances by the invading trees ran due east. Kimber brought the sled into line over it.

But it was a full hour before they reached the end of the forest and saw clearly the cracked and broken highway which was their guide. It threaded across open plains where now and again they sighted more of the dome dwellings standing alone and deserted, wreathed with masses of greenery.

"No people—the land is empty," Dard commented as the sled crossed the fourth of these."

"War," Kimber wondered, "or diseases. . . . Must have made a clean sweep in this section. And a long time ago —by the growth of the bushes and the appearance of the road."

It was more than two hours after they left the valley that they came upon what had been a village. And here was the first clue to the type of disaster which had struck the land. One vast pit was the center of the clustered domes. Crushed and shattered buildings ringed it, bearing the stains and melted smears of intense heat.

"Air raid?" Cully asked of the silence. "They got it good —and for keeps; it was war then."

Kimber did not circle the damage. Instead he stepped up the speed of the sled, driven by the same desire that possessed them all, the longing to know what lay beyond the broken horizon.

A second town, larger, brutally treated, its remaining structures half melted, its heart a crater, passed under them. Then again open country, beaded by deserted farms. The road ended at last in a city, shattered, smashed. A city planted on the shore of a bay, for here the sea curved in from the northwest to meet them once more.

There were towers, snapped, torn, twisted, until those in the sled could not be sure of their original shape, looming beside dark sores of craters. And at the waterside there was literally nothing but a slick expanse of crystalline slag reflecting the sun's rays.

Sea waves lipped that slag, but its edges remained unworn by the touch of water and time alike. And beyond, in the bay, the waves also curled restlessly about other wreckage—ships? Or parts of the buildings blown there?

Kimber cruised slowly across the spiderweb map of the ancient streets. But the wreckage was so complete they could only guess at the use or meaning of what they saw. Mounds of disintegrating metal might mark the residue of ground transportation devices, their weathered erosion testifying in part to the age of the disaster. And from the sled the explorers sighted nothing at all which might mark the remains of those who had lived there.

They landed on a patch of grassy ground before a huge pile of masonry which had three walls still standing. The ruined farmhouse had pictured for them tragedy, fear and cruelty. But this whole city—it was impersonal, too much. Such complete wreckage was closer to a dream.

"Atom bomb, H-bomb, Null-bomb." Cully recited the list of the worst Terra had known. "They must have had them here—all of them!"

"And they were certainly men—for they used them!" Kimber added savagely. He climbed out of the sled and faced the building. Its walls reflected the sun as if they were of some metallic substance but softly, with a glow of green-blue—as if the blocks used in building had been quarried of sea water. A flight of twelve steps, as wide as a Terran city block, led up to a mighty portal through which they could see the sun glow bright in the roofless interior.

Around that portal ran a band of colors, blending and contrasting in a queer way which might have had meaning and yet did not—for Terran eyes. As he studied the hues Dard thought he had a half-hint. Perhaps those colors did have a deliberate sequence—perhaps they were more than just decoration.

6. DISASTER

THEIR ATTEMPTS to explore on foot were frustrated by the mounds of debris and danger from falling rubble. Cully jumped to safety from the top of a mound which caved in under his weight, and so escaped a dangerous slide into one of the pits. Those pits were everywhere, dug so deeply into the foundations of the city that the Terrans, huddling on the ruins, could look down past several underground levels to a darkness uncut by the sun.

A little shaken by the engineer's narrow escape, they retired to the sled and made an unappetizing meal on concentrates.

"No birds," Dard suddenly realized that fact. "Nothing alive."

"Uhhuh." Santee dug his heel into the grass and earth. "No bugs either. And there're enough of them back in the valley!"

"No birds, no insects," Kimber said slowly. "The place is dead. I don't know how the rest of you feel, but I've had just about enough."

They did agree with that. The brooding stillness, broken only when debris crashed or rolled, rasped their nerves.

Dard swallowed his last bit of concentrate and turned to the pilot.

"Do we have any microfilm we can use?"

"For what—a lot of broken buildings?" Cully wanted to know.

"I'd like one of those bands of color around that doorway," Dard answered. His idea that the bands had a meaning was perhaps silly but he could not push it away.

"All right, kid." Kimber unpacked the small recorder and focused it on a place where the sun was strong. "No pattern I can see. But, it just might mean something at that."

That was the only picture they took when on the ground. But once again in the air Cully ran the machine for a bird's-eye view of as much of the ruined area as could be recorded.

They were approaching the outer reaches of the city to the east when Santee gave an exclamation and touched Kimber's arm. They were over a street less cumbered with rubble than any they had yet crossed, and there was a flicker of movement there.

As the sled coasted down they disturbed a pack of grayish, four-footed things that streaked away into the ruins leaving their meal behind them on the blood-smeared pavement.

"Whew!" Cully coughed and Dard gagged at the stench the wind carried in their direction. They left the sled to gather around the tangle of stripped bones and rotting flesh.

"That wasn't killed today," Kimber observed unnecessarily.

Dard rounded the stained area. The dead thing had been large, perhaps the size of a Terran draft horse, and the skeleton—tumbled as the bones now were—suggested that it was four-footed and hooved. But that skull, to which ragged and blood-clotted hair still clung, was what he had moved to see. He had been right—two horns sprouted above the eye sockets. This was the horned horse of the game set!"

"A duocorn?" mused the pilot.

"A what?" Santee wanted to know.

"There was a fabled animal mentioned in some of the old books on Terra. Had a single horn in the middle of the forehead, but the rest was all horse. Well, here's a horse with two horns—a duocorn instead of a unicorn. But those things we saw feeding here—they were pretty small to bring down an animal of this size."

"Unless they carry a burper, they didn't!" Dard, in spite of the odor, leaned down to inspect that stretch of spine beyond the loose skull. A section of vertebra had been smashed just as if a giant vise had been applied to the nape of the duocorn's neck.

"Crushed!" Kimber agreed. "But whatever could do that?"

Cully studied the body. "Mighty big for a horse."

"There were breeds on earth which were seventeen to twenty hands high at the shoulder and weighed close to a ton," returned Kimber. "This fellow must have been about that size."

"And what is big enough to crunch through a spine supporting a ton of meat?" Santee wanted to know. He went back to the sled and picked up the rifle.

Dard back-trailed from the evil-smelling bones. Several paces farther on he discovered what he was looking for, marks which proved that the body had been dragged and worried for almost half of a city block. And also, plain to reach in a drift of soil across the street, prints. The marks cut deeply by the hooves of the duocorn were half blotted out in places by another spoor—three long-clawed toes, with faint scuffed spaces between, as if they were united by a webbed membrane. Dard went down on one knee and flexed his own hand over the clearest of those prints. With his fingers spread to the fullest extent he could just span it.

"Looks like a chicken track." Santee had come up behind him.

"More likely a reptile. I've seen a field lizard leave a spoor such as this—except for the size."

"Another dragon—large size?" Cully suggested.

149

Dard shook his head as he got to his feet and started along that back trail. "This one runs, not flies. But I'm sure it's a nasty customer."

There was a scuttling to their left. Santee whirled, rifle ready. A small stone rolled from the top of the nearest pile of rubbish and thudded home against the yellow teeth of the skull.

"Somebody's getting impatient over an interrupted dinner." Cully ended with a laugh which sounded unnaturally loud in these surroundings.

Kimber went back to the sled. "We might as well let him—or her—or it—come back to the table. There are," he glanced around at the ruins, "altogether too many good lurking places here. I'll feel safer out in open country where I can see any lizard that big—before it sees me!"

But when they were air borne Kimber did not turn inland, instead he followed the curve of the bay on to the northwest. The ruins beneath them dwindled to isolated houses—domed or towered—in better repair than those situated in the heart of the city. Beneath them now were brilliant patches of flowers long since returned to the wild. Little streams made graceful curves through what Dard was sure had been pleasure gardens. Fairy towers, which appeared too delicate to withstand the pull of the planet's gravity, pointed useless fingers up at the cruising sled.

Once they flew for almost half a mile above a palace. But here again a curdled crystalline blotch cut the building in two. None of what they saw gave them any desire to descend and explore. Here the trees grew too high, there were too many shadows. The tangled pleasure gardens and wild grounds were good lurking places for terror to stalk the unwary.

The broken city faded into the green of the rolling country and the aquamarine of the sea. Fewer and fewer domed houses broke the green—and those were probably farms. Here were birds as if the haunted horror of the city was gone. The seashore curved again but Kimber did not follow it west. He veered to the east, to cross fields of which the old regular patterns were marked by bushy hedgerows. It was in one of these that they sighted the first living duo-corns, four adults and two colts, but all four well under the size of the monster whose skeleton had attracted their attention in the city.

These animals were uniform in color, showing none of the variations in marking possessed by Terran horses. Their coats were a slaty blue-gray, their unkempt manes and tails black, and their bellies and the under portions of their legs silver. The horns were silver with the real sheen of the precious metal.

As the sled droned over them, the largest flung up its head to issue a trumpeting scream. Then, herding its companions before it, it settled into a rocking gallop up the sloping field to the hedge at the far side beyond which was a grove of trees. With graceful ease all of the fleeing animals leaped the hedge and disappeared under those trees, nor did they come out on the other side of the grove.

"Good runners," Cully gave credit. "Do you suppose they were always wild—or the descendants of domestic stock? Bet Harmon'd like to have a couple of them. He was pretty fed up when he found we couldn't bring those two colts he had picked out."

"The big one was a fighter! D'yuh see him shake them horns?" demanded Santee. "I wouldn't want him to catch me out in the open walkin'."

"Odd." Dard had been watching the far end of the grove and was now puzzled. "You'd think they'd keep on running. But they're staying in there."

"Under cover. Safe from any menace from the air," Kimber said. "Which suggests some unpleasant possibilities."

"A large flying danger!" Dard whistled as he caught Kimber's idea. "A thing maybe as big as this sled. But it would be too big to fly on its own power!"

"Bigger things than this have flown in Terra's past," the pilot reminded him. "And it may not be a living thing they fear—but a machine. Either way—we'd better watch out."

"But those flying things were far back in our history,"

protested the boy. "Could such primitive things exist along with man—or whatever built that city?"

"How can we say what may or may not have survived here? Or—if that city was destroyed by radioactive missiles —what may have mutated? Or what may fly machines?"

Since the duocorns remained stubbornly in hiding, the sled gave up investigation and flew east, the setting sun behind them and long afternoon shadows stretching to point their path.

"Where we gonna camp?" Santee wanted to know. "Out here somewheres?"

"I'd say yes," Kimber said. "There's a river over there. Might find a good place somewhere along it."

The river was shallow and its waters were clear enough for them to be able to sight from the air the rough stones which paved its bed. An uneven fringe of water plants cloaked the shore line until climbing ground provided bluffs. The sparkle of sun on ripples flashed up from a wider expanse as the sled reached a place where the graveled bed flattened out into a round lake. The stream spattered down from heights to feed this, forming a miniature water- fall, and there was a level stretch of sand unencumbered by rocks which made a good landing for the sled.

Cully stretched and grinned. "Good enough. You know how to pick 'em, Sim. Even a cave to sleep in!"

The space he pointed to was not a real cave, rather a semiprotected hollow beneath an overhang of rock. But it gave them a vague sense of security when they unrolled their sleeping bags against its back wall.

This was the first night Dard had spent in the open under a moonless sky and he found the darkness discomforting— though stars made new crystal patterns across the heavens. They had a fire of river drift, but beyond that the darkness was thick enough to be smooth between thumb and fore- finger.

The fire had died down to gleaming coals when Dard was shocked awake by a howling wail. The sound was re- peated, to be either echoed or answered from down river. Above the rumble of the fall he was sure he caught the clink of disturbed gravel. Another ear-splitting shriek made his heart jump as Kimber flashed on the beam of a pocket torch without moving from beside him.

Pinned in that beam hunched a weird biped. About four feet tall, its body was completely covered with fine silky hair which arose in a fluff along its back and limbs, roughened by its astonished fright. The face was three-quarters eyes, round, staring, with no discernible lids. There was no apparent nose above an animal's sharply fanged muzzle. Four-digit hands went up to shield those eyes and the thing gave a moan which arose to a howl. But it made no attempt to flee, as if the strange light held it prisoner.

"Monkey!" that was Santee. "A night runnin' monkey!"

Into that beam from the torch, insects began to gather—great feathery-winged moth things, some as large as birds. And, at their appearance, the night howler came to life. With a feline's lithe grace it leaped and captured two of the moths and then scurried into the darkness where a low snarl suggested that it was now disputing possession of these prizes with another. Kimber held the torch steady and the moths came in, a drifting cloud, coasting along that ray toward the explorers. Round eyeballs of phosphorescence glittered just on the border of that light. And furry paws clawed through it at the flying things. Triumphant squeaks heralded captures and the howling arose in a triumphant chorus as if others were being summoned to this lucky hunting. Kimber snapped off the light just before the first wave of moths reached the Terrans.

The whisper of wings was drowned out by several shrill cries. But when the light was not turned on again the four heard the rattle of gravel and a fading wailing as the "monkeys" withdrew down river.

"Show's over for this night—I hope," Cully grunted sleepily. "Bet some wise guy could make a fortune selling torches to those boys as moth lures."

Dard allowed his head to drop back on the padded end of the sleeping bag. Suppose those "monkeys" were intelligent enough to enable the Terrans to establish trade relations. Could one make contact with them? To the human eye their manlike stance and the way they used their hands made them appear more approachable than any other native creatures of this world which the Terrans had so far sighted. Surely these creatures had not built the city. But they walked erect and had been quick enough to evaluate the use of light for attracting their food supply. If they were wholly night creatures, as their large eyes and ease in traveling through the dark suggested, would the Terrans ever see them again?

Dard was still puzzling that out when he slipped into a dream in which he again stood before the ruined building within the city and studied those baffling lines of color. But this time those bands held a meaning, and he had almost grasped it when he heard a sound behind him. Not daring to turn his head—for he knew that death sniffed his trail—he began to run with dragging, leaden feet. And, behind him, death pounded relentlessly. With bursting lungs he turned the corner into another cluttered, half-blocked street and saw before him blood and bones from which gray things ran. He slipped, went down. . . . He awoke, his heart pounding wildly, his body slippery with a dank, chill sweat. It was gray light. He could see the moving water, the remains of the previous night's fire. Stealthily he wriggled out of his sleeping bag and crawled in to the open.

Then he went to the water and splashed it over head and forearms, until its clear chill washed out of him the fear the nightmare had left. Gasping a little from the chill he tramped along to the rising cliffs beside the falls.

Vines ran down the shiny black of this stone, clinging to its uneven surface with tiny sucker feet. The lianas themselves were a gray-white and bare of leaves except for a few which grew in tight bunches near the top of the cliff. Clusters of ropy creepers dangled in a limp fringe along each main stem.

In a pocket formed by the crossing of several lianas he sighted a find. Surely that brighter green marked one of the perfume plants Trude Harmon wanted! The triangular leaves, glossy and colorful against such a drab background, bobbed from scarlet stems. And there were seed pods also! They hung, red and yellow, pulled down by the weight of their contents, within his reach. He snapped off three and stretched to reach a fourth.

It was just then he caught sight of the twitching close to the ground, where something struggled hopelessly. Two of the creepers, about the size of his little finger, were holding in a throttling grip the writhing body of a hopper. The small animal's eyes protruded agonizingly and a bloody froth ringed its gasping mouth. Dard drew his knife and slashed at the white cords. But the steel did not cut through them. It rebounded as if he had tried to sever rubber with a dull edge. Before he could raise it for a second blow, a larger creeper flicked out and encircled his wrist, pulling him off balance against the cliff. With lightning speed the ropy fringe dangling there came to life, those near enough whipping over his body, those too far away straining toward the struggle until they were stretched in straight lines. And, as each tie fell about him, he discovered that it was equipped with small thorns which tore his skin in red-hot torment. He shouted and fought, but all his struggles seemed to carry him closer to other suckers and they were fast winding him helpless when he heard the excited cries of the others and saw them racing for him.

Before they were close enough to help he was able to tear his knife arm free, to slash and score the mass of weaving tendrils which enclosed him. Then he paused—the things were falling away of their own accord. Within another minute the last and largest sullenly relinquished its hold.

"What happened?" yelled Santee. "What did you do to make those things let go?"

Wherever the plants had met his flesh they had left their brand in pin-point dots of oozing blood which trickled down his arms, throat and one cheek. But those lianas which had fallen away from him—they were turning black, shriveling, rotting away in pieces! The thing had tasted his blood and it was poisoned!

"Poisoned! I poisoned it!"

"Be glad that you did," snapped Kimber. "You're in luck. These weren't!" He kicked up the gravel below the vines with the toe of his boot and plowed up brittle bones and small skulls.

The pilot as he treated Dard's slight wounds was emphatic:

"Hereafter we stay together. It worked out all right this time. But again it might not. Stick together and distrust everything unless you have already seen it in action!"

But they were all together and apparently in no danger when disaster struck them a back-handed blow that same day. They had been using the sleepy stream as a guide back into a range of hills and by midmorning had sighted in the northeast what could only be a chain of mountains, purple-blue against the sky. These ran from north to south as far as those in the sled could see.

Perhaps if the Terrans had not been so intent upon those distant peaks they might have seen something below which would have warned them. Probably not. Man, when he goes to war, displays the deepest depths of cunning.

The first intimation of danger arrived simultaneously with the blow that smashed them out of the sky. A sharp burst of sound and the sled bucked—as if batted by a giant club. The craft fluttered into a falling twirl while Kimber fought the controls, trying to pull out of the spin. If the passengers had not been strapped in they would have plunged earthward in the first three seconds of that wild descent.

While Dard was trying to understand what had happened a burst of brilliant light temporarily blinded him. More sound, bracketing them, and someone cried out in pain. Then he knew that they were falling out of control, and by some instinct he flung up his arms to shield his head just before they struck and he blacked out.

He couldn't have been unconscious long, because when he raised his head Cully was still dazedly fumbling to free himself from the safety straps. Dard spat to clear a full mouth and saw a blob of blood and a tooth strike the ground. He loosened the belt and lurched out of the sled after Cully. In front Santee bent over a limp Kimber on whose face blood trickled from a cut just below the hair line.

"What happened?" Dard wiped his chin and took away a bloody hand. His lips hurt and his jaw ached.

Kimber's dark eyes opened and stared up at them bemusedly. Then comprehension came back and he demanded:

"Who shot us down?"

Santee had his rifle in his hands.

"That's what I'm gonna see, right now!"

Before the rest could protest, he darted away, back down the valley where they had landed, zigzagging into cover as he neared its mouth. There was a final boom of an exploding shell from that direction and then silence.

Dard and Cully got Kimber free of the sled. The pilot's right arm was bleeding from a ragged wound near the shoulder. They broke open the medical kit and the engineer went competently to work so that Dard had nothing to do. When Kimber was stretched out on a bedroll Cully returned to examine the sled itself. He took up the cover of the motor and squirmed half into the space which enclosed it, ordering Dard to hold the torch for him. When he crawled back his face was very sober.

"How bad?" asked Kimber. There was more color in his dark face and he levered himself up on an elbow.

"Not the worst—but about as near to that as we can get." Cully was interrupted by a shout from the trees where Santee had disappeared.

The big man returned walking in the open, his rifle cradled in the crook of his arm—as if they had nothing to fear.

"Fellas, this here's plain crazy! There's a nest of guns down there all hidden away. Little stuff—light field pieces. But there's not a livin' critter in the place. Them there guns fired at us their ownselves!"

"A robot control triggered when we flew over a certain

point!" exploded Cully. "Some kind of radar, I'll bet. Rogan ought to be here."

"First," Kimber reminded him grimly, "we've got to get back to tell him about them."

A broken sled with which to cross several hundred miles of unknown country. They were going to have quite a hike, thought Dard. But he did not comment upon that aloud.

7.   RETURN JOURNEY

"WONDER HOW MANY more booby traps such as that are hidden around?" Cully glanced down the valley with open suspicion.

"Not many, I'd say," Kimber answered weakly. "It must have been only a fluke that those guns were still able to fire—"

His voice was swallowed by an explosion severe enough to rock the ground under them. Dard saw earth, trees and debris rise into the air far down the valley as an acrid white-yellow smoke fouled the air in drifting wisps.

"That," Kimber said into the ensuing silence, "was probably the end of the guns. They've blown themselves up."

"Shoulda done that sooner!" growled Santee. "A lot sooner! How about us gettin' away from here?" He turned to Cully who had been blasted loose from his work on the sled.

"That's going to be a problem. She'll get into the air again, yes. But not with a full load. Stripped down she may be able to carry two—flying with a list."

Santee grinned at his fellow castaways. "All right. Two of us'll hike and pack some stuff. The other two'll ride."

Kimber frowned as he agreed reluctantly. "I suppose we'll have to do that. Those in the sled can make a camp a half day's march ahead and wait for the others to catch up. We mustn't lose contact. Do you think you can raise Rogan in the valley?"

Cully brought out the small vedio. And Kimber, using his left hand awkwardly, made the proper adjustment. But there was no answering spark. The engineer raised the box and shook it gently. They all heard that faint answering rattle which put an end to their hopes of a message to those they had left by the sea.

Camp was made that night just where the fortunes of that long ago war had marooned them. Santee and Dard undertook another visit to the hidden emplacement. Two of the strange guns were tilted at a crazy angle, their loading mechanism ripped wide open, behind them a pit, newly hollowed and still cloudy with fumes.

Keeping away from that the two Terrans prowled about the installation. If man or any other intelligent life had been there before them, it had been many years in the past. But Dard, knowing very little of mechanics, believed that it had been robot controlled. Perhaps lack of man-power had made the last war a purely push-button affair.

"Now here's somethin'!"

Santee's shout brought him to an opening in the ground. The cover had been wrenched loose by the explosion and its clever camouflage no longer hid the steps leading down into the dark. Santee flashed a beam ahead and started to descend. The steps were very narrow and shallow as if those who had used them had had feet not quite the same shape or size of a Terran's. But once down, the explorers found themselves in a square box of a metal-walled chamber. Along one entire wall was a control panel and facing it a small table and a single backless bench. Otherwise the room was empty.

"Musta jus' set them robots goin' and left. This metal ain't rusted none. But it was left a long time ago. . . ."

As Santee swept the light across that control board Dard saw an object lying on the table. He picked up his find just as the big man started up the stairs to the outer and fresher air.

What he held was four sheets of a crystalline substance, fastened together at the upper left-hand corner. Running through each sheet, as if they had been embedded when the stuff was made, were lines of shaded colors in combinations not unlike those he had seen about the city door. Instruction book? Orders? Did Those Others express their thoughts in color patterns? He thrust the find into his safest pocket, determined to compare it with the microfilm of the doorway.

The next morning they followed Santee's plan. The pilot, handicapped by a stiff shoulder, went in the sled along with Cully who was able to take the controls. Their supplies pared to the minimum were shared between the sled and two packs for Dard and Santee.

When the sled took off, due south, it cruised just above tree-top level. It would fly at lowest speed on that same course until noon when its crew would camp, waiting for the two on foot to join them.

Dard shouldered his pack, setting it into place with a weight, and picked up their compass. Santee followed with pack and rifle, and they went forward at a ground-eating pace Dard had learned in the woods of Terra, as the sled vanished over the rise.

For the most part they found the going through this rolling country easy. There were no wooded stretches to form impassable barriers, and they soon struck an old road running in the right direction to provide footing good enough to allow a faster pace. Insects spun out of the tall grass to blunder past them and hoppers spied them constantly.

Shortly before noon the road made a sharp curve west toward the distant sea, and the Terrans had to strike away across fields again. They had the good luck to stumble on a farm where not only one but two of the golden apple trees bent under the weight of ripe fruit. Pushing through the mob of semidrunk birds, insects, and hoppers, including a new and larger variety of the latter, they secured fruit which was not only food but drink, filling an improvised bag for the sake of the sled riders.

Santee bit into the fragrant pulp with a sigh of pleasure.

"D'yuh know—I wonder a lot—where did all the people go? They had a bad war—sure. But there must have been *some* survivors. Everybody couldn't have been killed!"

"What if they used gas, or a germ—certain kinds of infective radiation?" questioned Dard. "There are no traces of any survivors, in the city ruins, around farms."

"It looks to me jus' as if"—the big rifleman licked his fingers carefully—"they all packed up and got out together, the way we left the Cleft."

When they left the farm the character of the country began to change. Here the soil was spotted with patches of sandy gravel which grew larger. The clumps of trees dwindled to thickets of wiry thorn bushes, and there were outcroppings of the same shiny black rock which had nursed the killing vines by the river. Santee shot a long survey about as they halted on the top of a steep hill.

"This's kinda like a desert. Glad we brought them apples—we might not hit water here."

It was hot, hotter than it had seemed back when they were in the blue-green fields, for this sun-baked red-brown earth and blue sand reflected the heat. Dard's skin, chafed by the pack straps, smarted when moisture trickled down between his shoulder blades. He licked his lips and tasted salt. Santee's comment concerning lack of water had aroused his thirst.

Below them was a gorge. Dard blinked and rubbed his eyes with the back of his hand. No, that was no trick of shimmering heat—there was a bright gleaming line straight across the floor of the valley. He called it to Santee's attention and the other focused the field glasses on it.

"A rail! But why only one?"

"We can get down over there," Dard pointed. "Let's see what it is."

They made the hard climb down to verify the fact that a single metal rail did reach from one tunnel hole in the gorge wall to another tunnel directly across. Unable to discover anything else, they pulled themselves up the opposite cliff to continue the southward march.

It was midafternoon when they saw, rising into a cloudless sky, the smoke signal of the sled. And their strides became a trot until they panted up the side of a small mesa-plateau to the camp.

"How long," Santee wanted to know later as they sucked appreciatively on golden apples, "is this trip gonna last?"

"Another full day's journey for you two, and maybe half the next. At this speed we can't expect to cut it any shorter," Kimber replied. "Jorge's been working on the engine again. But there isn't much he can do without other tools."

The big man grinned. "Well, these here plasta-boots of our'n are holdin' up pretty well. We can keep sloggin' a while longer. And there's nothin' to be afraid of."

"Don't be too sure of that," cautioned the pilot. "Keep your eyes open, you two. There may have been other booby booby traps scattered around. Since we were shot down, traps scattered around. Since we were shot down, I don't trust even a clear sky!"

The second day's routine followed the first. Except, in the arid desert land, it was tougher going and they did not make time.

Dard's head went up and his nostrils expanded as he started to pick his way down a series of ledges into a sandy-floored ravine. There was a musky, highly repellent stench arising from below. And he had sniffed something very much like it before! The putrescent remains of the duocorn! Below, an organic thing was very dead! Santee worked along to join him.

"What're you stoppin' for?"

"Smell that?"

Santee's bearded face wrinkled. "Yah, a big stink! Somethin' dead!"

Dard studied the ground before them carefully. If they tried to double back on their trail through this up and down country they were going to lose hours of time. After all, what had made that kill below—if it were a kill—might have been gone for days. He decided to leave it up to Santee.

"Shall we go down?"

"We'll lose a lotta time back trailin' from here. I'd say keep on."

But they continued the descent cautiously and when Dard disturbed a small stone, which dropped noisily over the edge, he stiffened for several listening seconds. There was no sound from below—nothing but that terrible stomach-disturbing odor.

Santee unslung the rifle, and Dard's hand went to his own belt. That morning Cully had given him the ray gun, suggesting that it could be of more use to the foot travelers. Now, as his hand closed around the butt, Dard was very glad that he held it. There was something about this ill-omened place—something in the very silence which brooded there—that hinted of danger.

A screen of stubby thorn bushes masked the far end of the narrow ravine, hinting at the presence of moisture, although the prickly leaves had a grayish, unhealthy cast.

The two worked their way through these as carefully and noiselessly as possible and found a seeping spring. Minerals salted the lip of the water-filled depression, and a greenish powder was dry along the banks of the rivulet which trickled on down the valley.

Chemical fumes from the water scented the air, but not heavy enough to cover the other sickish effluvium.

They should have beaten their way through the brush to the other side of the valley and climbed out of that tainted hole. But no broken ledges hung over there to furnish climbing aids, and they followed the stream along in the search for an easier path.

The contaminated water spilled out into a shallow stinking pool with a broad rim of the poisonous green.

Grouped around the far perimeter of the pool, half buried in the sand, were such things as nightmares are made of!

Their dingy yellowish-green skins were scaled with the stigmata of the reptile. But the creatures drowsing in the sun were not even as wholesome as the snakes most humans shrink from with age-old inbred horror. These were true monsters—evil. Gorged, they had fallen in a stupor among the grisly fragments of their feasting, and from those fragments and the smeared sand came a stench foul enough to suggest that this was a long used lair.

Dard estimated that they were from seven to ten feet long. The hind legs, ending in huge webbed feet, mere stems of bone laced with powerful driving muscles. Short, horribly stained forearms had terrible travesties of human hands which curved over their protruding bellies, each finger a ten-inch claw. But their heads were the worst, too small for the bodies, flat of skull, they were mounted on unusually long and slender necks, giving the impression of a cobra on the shoulders of a lizard.

As the two humans halted, a flap of loose skin on the belly of the nearest nightmare was pushed aside and a small replica of the monster drew itself out of a sac and wobbled weakly down to the water, curling its neck over to suck up the liquid. After it swallowed the first mouthful, some instinct drew its attention to the watchers. With a shrill hiss it scrambled back to its parent. The head of the larger thing snapped up, swaying back and forth, a snake preparing to strike!

Dard threw himself back, carrying Santee with him. They were brought up short by the cliff wall, but they dared not turn their backs upon the aroused monster long enough to find hand and foot holds there.

The thing across the pool was on its feet, towering far over them. With a cuff of one paw it sent the infant sprawling to safety before it slewed around kicking up blood-clotted sand. The flat serpent's head went down to a level with the lizardlike shoulders, and from its fanged jaws came a hiss which gathered volume until it rivaled the piercing whistle of a steam-powered engine.

That battle cry aroused its fellow sleepers. But they arose sluggishly, too torpid from their feasting to respond.

Santee shot. The nerve-paralyzing projectile of the stun rifle struck fair between those murderous yellow, unwinking eyes. The skull shattered with a spatter of green ooze. But the thing waded the pool to rush them, tearing claws outstretched. It should have been dead. But with a broken, empty skull, blinded, it came on!

"No brain in the head!" Dard shouted. "Jump!"

They jumped apart. The advancing horror struck hard against the cliff to cling there stubbornly clawing at the rock. It continued to scream senselessly, bringing the others of its kind into full alertness.

One gave a bound, clearing the pool, to fall upon its wounded companion with tearing jaws and claws. The other three appeared undecided. Their snake heads rose and fell as they hissed. One made to join the battle on the other side of the pool and then retreated.

Daring to hesitate no longer, Dard took careful aim with the ray gun and sent a green beam straight into the distended middle of the creature that rocked from one splayed foot to another on his right. The Terrans had to clear a path past the pool, for to return near the fighters was sure death.

Screaming madly, Dard's quarry clapped both hands over the frightful gapping emptiness the ray had left and wilted forward into the water, sending up a slimy spray of blood and poisonous liquid. With the attention of its two fellows attracted to its struggles Dard darted to join Santee.

Together the humans edged along the cliff wall, their goal the valley beyond the pool. For a few minutes it seemed that they might be able to gain it undetected by the monsters. For one of the unhurt creatures had gone to work on the body in the pool. But when its smaller companion made to join it, fangs and talons threatened, forcing that other to withdraw, hissing fury. As its head swung back and forth it sighted the Terrans. An arching leap brought it after them. Both the length and speed of that bound panicked the cornered men. They scrambled into the meager protection offered by the boulders and fallen rock. Santee's second bullet tore a hole in the scaled breast of the pursuer without slowing its charge. Dard pressed the firing stud on the ray gun. But the responding beam was weak. It clipped the side of the weaving head, shearing off part of the skull and one eye, and cutting neck muscles so badly that the battered head flopped erratically.

Dard fired again—with no result. The clip left in the weapon must have been exhausted! His ears roared as Santee shot from beside him. But the bullet only nicked the shoulder of the writhing body. Despairing they scuttled and backed away, keeping in among the rough footing. But they were past the pool, in the middle of the valley, on a course which paralleled a path worn deep and smooth by the feet of the monsters.

The scream of the hunter behind them was cut by a trumpeting squeal. A second was bearing down to join in the chase.

"Ahead—three—four—yards"—Dard got out the words between tearing breaths—"hole—too—small——"

He concentrated on reaching that haven, and Santee ran beside him. The hole was a perfectly round one, and from it ran the monorail of the ancient transport system. They threw themselves into the dark, scrambling on until Dard brought up against a heavy object which gave under his weight, slipping on so suddenly that he sprawled face down, the wind driven out of him.

When he caught his breath again he sat up, still groggy. The crack of the rifle filled the tunnel with a blast of sound.

"Got one at last! And it's blocked up that hole—for a while anyways. But it ain't healthy in here—they can get in—squeeze themselves altogether and do it. What the—!" The big man ended his report with an exclamation of both outrage and fear.

Dard had breath enough to ask: "What's the matter?"

"That was the last round, I just fired. You got another clip for the ray gun?"

"No."

"Then we'd better make tracks for the other end of this here tunnel. From the sound back there they're taking the dead one out—in pieces! When they've got that done they'll be after us again'——"

"Let's have the flash. There's something ahead here. It moves——"

Dard put a tentative hand out—to encounter the smoothness of metal. And when Santee snapped on the torch beam he discovered that he was fronting a cylinder, not unlike the one they had pulled out of the seaside tube. But this one was mounted on a grooved fin made to run along the monorail. There was no way of getting past it, since its sides were within inches of the tunnel walls. They would have to push it before them if they were going to get out the other end.

That worked properly for about five minutes and then an extra hard push sent the carrier ahead to stop with a clang. All their shoving force could force it along no farther. Dard flattened himself against the wall and flashed the torch down the side of the cylinder.

"There's a cave-in!"

Santee massaged his bearded chin with a dirt-streaked hand. "Kinda bottles us up, don't it? Give us the light and let's have a look along these walls."

Several paces back he found a niche, not too roomy and still accommodating some oddly shaped tools which Santee kicked aside.

"Repairman's safety hole," he explained. "Thought maybe we might happen on one of these here. Now, suppose we work that there truck past here and get ahead to look at the damage."

Pushing the carrier before them had been an easy task. But getting it back again was another matter altogether, especially when there were no proper handholds on its smooth surface. As they worked at it, hampered by their necessarily cramped position, they broke nails and tore fingers raw. The stubborn thing moved with frustrating slowness. While, to rasp the nerves, sounds from the entrance told them that the body which had obstructed passage there was being rapidly disposed of.

At last the car was pushed far enough along so that they could get out of the niche behind it. Without waiting to take up their packs, they ran to the cave-in, only to be met by a hard mound of earth and rock. Santee dug the barrel of his rifle into it, disturbing only a scattered clod or two. To dig a way through that they needed tools, and time—and they had neither as the big man was forced to acknowledge.

"There're two of them critters left. And if either one gets in here now it's gonna push that car right back on us. But—if there's any smashin' done—I'm gonna be the one to do it!"

He padded purposefully back to the carrier. Dard hurried after him. The picture Santee had evoked, of the lizard things pushing that car down upon *them*, was one he didn't want to think about. He had no idea of what Santee had in mind, but any action now was better than just waiting for such an end.

"All right," Santee put his hands on the back of the carrier, "put away that torch and start pushin'! Here's where we give them lizards a big surprise—a nasty one, too, I hope!"

Dard dropped the torch and put his hands beside Santee's. Together they set their strength against the immobility of the carrier. It moved, much more easily than it had before. There was a low hum which became a steady purr. It gathered speed—moving away from them.

"We've started it to workin'!" Santee's exultant cry arose to explain. He caught Dard and held him away from the entrance as the carrier sped on.

There was a shock of impact followed by a hissing scream. Then they saw the clear circle of daylight marking the entrance, carrier and besiegers were both gone!

8.   DESSIE'S MERMAN

WHEN NOTHING moved across that circle of light, they dared to retrieve their packs and go out.

The carrier had plunged full speed ahead, leaving the curve of the monorail. Under it, but crushed legs pinned to the sand and rock of the valley floor, threshed one of the monsters, writhing over the torn remains of the one Santee had shot earlier. Leaping out of the reach of the prisoned creature's darting head the Terrans rounded its body and made for the opposite wall of the canyon.

Here the rock afforded holds and they pulled themselves up. But the lizard crushed beneath the car appeared to be alone and nothing menaced their retreat. Panting, they reached the top and dared to look back.

Below, the monster still fought insanely against the carrier which held it down. But if there were others of its fellows alive they had not joined it. Santee wiped his steaming face with the back of a hand.

"I still don't know how we got outa that one, kid. It was sure a close call."

"Too close. I want to catch up to the sled before we run into any more of those murdering devils."

"Yeah," Santee pulled ruefully at the sling of the rifle. "Next time I go walkin', I'm gonna have a lotta ammo. This here country's got too many surprises."

They set out at a sober pace, too exhausted by their exertions of the past hour to hurry. It was dusk growing into night before they found their way down a rise into another grassy plain. In the distance was a massed shadow of what could only be a wood.

Would they have to fight their way through or around that, Dard asked himself drearily. But a light reassured him. There was a campfire down there. Cully had landed the sled this side of the barrier.

As Santee and Dard dragged themselves wearily into the circle of firelight they were met with a flood of questions. Dard was too tired to try to answer. He ate and drank and crawled into his bedroll before all the tale of their adventure of the afternoon had been told. Kimber was very sober when it was complete.

"That was too close. We'll have to go better armed when we explore. But now that we know there is no civilized threat to our colony it may be some time before we return this way. Tomorrow the sled will ferry us over the forest and the cliffs and we shall be home. Those *are* our cliffs there."

"Home," Dard repeated that word in his mind, trying to associate it with the sea valley, with the cave house of the star voyagers. A long, long time ago "home" had had a good meaning. Before the burning, before the purge. But his memory of that halcyon time was so dim. Then "home" had meant the farm, and cold, hunger, the constant threat of danger. Now "home" would be a cell hollowed out of a colored cliff on a weird world generations of time away from Terra.

In the morning he lazed about the camp with Santee while Cully, after a last tune-up of the limping engine, lifted the sled toward the sea with Kimber as the first passenger. It was an hour before the sled returned and the engineer ordered Dard into the listing craft. They flew slowly, skimming the barrier, and Cully did not take him all the way down the sea valley to the cliff house, but dropped him with his pack at the edge of the ancient fields.

Dard swished through the tall grass. He could see people moving in the distant fields, more of them than had been about when he had left. More of the sleepers had probably been aroused.

Then a clear, lilting whistle announced the boy, some years younger than himself, who came driving before him three calves. He stopped short when he caught sight of the battered explorer and smiled.

"Hi! You're Dard Nordis, ain't you? Say, you musta had yourself a time—seein' them ruined cities and the lizards and all! I'm gonna go out and see 'em, too—when I can get Dad to let me. I'm Lanny Harmon. Can you wait 'til I stake out these critters? I'd like to go back with you."

"Sure." Dard eased his pack to the ground and watched Lanny tether the calves in the pasture.

"They sure do like this kinda grass," the farm boy explained as he came back. "Hey, let me carry that there pack for you. Mr. Kimber said you had a big fight with some giant lizards. Are they worse'n those flyin' dragons?"

170

"They sure are," Dard replied feelingly. "Say, is everybody awake now?"

"Everybody's that's goin' to." A shadow darkened the boy's face for a moment. "Six didn't come through. Dr. Skort—but you knew 'bout him, and Miz Winson, and Miz Grene, Looie Denton and a coupla men I didn't know. But the rest, they're all right. We were awful lucky. Whee—look out!"

Dard overbalanced as he tried to stop in mid-step and landed on the ground beside Lanny who had squatted down to sweep away the grass and display a dome of mud-plastered leaves and grass.

"What in the world?"

Lanny chuckled. "That there's a hopper house! Dessie, she found one yesterday and showed me where to look. Watch!" He rapped smartly with his knuckles on the top of the dome.

A second later a hopper's head popped out of the ground level door and the indignant beast let them know very plainly its opinion of such a disturbance of the peace.

"Dessie, she got a hopper to stand still and let her pet him. My sister Marya—now she wants a hopper—says they're like kittens. But Ma says they steal too much and we ain't gonna bring any in the cave. I'd like to try to tame one though."

They detoured around a field of the blue-pod grain, meeting the harvesters working there. Dard shook hands with strangers, bewildered by all the new faces. As he went on he asked Lanny:

"How many are there of us now?"

Lanny's lips moved as he counted. "Twenty-five men—counting you explorers—and twenty-three women. Then there're the girls, my sisters, Marya and Martie, and Dessie and Lara Skort—they're all little. And Don Winson, he's just a baby. That's all. Most of the men are down rippin' up the ship."

"Ripping up the ship?" Why did that dismay him so?

"Sure. We ain't gonna fly again—not enough fuel. And

she was made to take apart so we can use parts of her for machine shops and things like that. Well—here we are!"

They came out on what was now a well-defined path running up to the main entrance of the cave. Three men were working on a swinging platform suspended from the top of the cliff, fitting glass into a hole ready to receive it as a window.

"Dardie! Dardie! Dardie!"

A whirlwind swept down upon him, wrapping thin arms about his waist, burrowing a face against him. He went down on his knees and took Dessie into a tight hug.

"Dardie," she was sniffling a little. "They said you would come an' I've been watching all the time! Dardie," she smiled at him blissfully, "I do like this place! I do! There are lots of animals in the grass and some of them have houses just like us—and they like me! Now that you've come home, Dardie, everything is wonderful—truly it is!"

"It sure is, honey."

"So there you are, son," Trude Harmon bore down upon him. "Hungry, too, I'll wager. You come right in and rest and eat. Heard tell that you had yourselves some excitin' times."

With Dessie holding his hand tightly and Lanny bringing up the rear still carrying his pack, Dard came into a room where there was a long table flanked by benches. Kimber was already sitting there, empty plates before him, talking to an excited Kordov.

"But where did they go—those city dwellers?" the little biologist sputtered as Dard waded into the food Trude Harmon spread before him. "They could not just vanish—pouff!" He snapped his fingers. "As if they were but puffs of smoke!"

Kimber gave the same answer to that question as Dard had made. "Say an epidemic following war—germ warfare—or radiation sickness—who can tell now? By the weathering of the city they have been gone a long time. We found no traces of anything but animal life. And nothing to fear but the lizards . . ."

"A whole world deserted!" Kordov shook his head. "It

is enough to frighten one! Those Others took the wrong turning somewhere."

"It is up to us to see that we don't follow their example," Kimber cut in.

That evening the voyagers gathered about a giant campfire in the open space before the cliff house, while Kimber and the others in turn recited the saga of their journey into the interior. The city, the robot-controlled battery, the battle with the lizards, held their listeners enthralled. But when they had done the question came again:

"But where *did* they go?"

Kordov gave the suggested answers, but then he added: "It would be better if we asked ourself now *why* did they go and be governed by the reply to that. They have left us a deserted land in which to make a new beginning. Though we must not forget that in other continents of this world some remnants of that race may still exist. Wisdom suggests alertness in the future."

Dessie, sitting in Dard's lap, leaned her head back against his shoulder and whispered:

"I like hearing about the night monkeys, Dardie. Do you suppose they will ever come here so I can see them too? Knowing them would be fun."

"Yes, it would," he whispered back.

Maybe someday when they were sure of safety beyond the cliffs, all the Terrans could venture out and he could show Dessie the night monkeys. But not until the last of that scaled death had been found and exterminated!

Since Kimber could not use his arm until the shoulder wound healed, Dard became hands for the pilot, working with Cully on the damaged sled. Seeing that he could and did follow instructions, Cully went back to his own pet project of dismantling the engine of the carrier they had rescued from the sea tube. He intended some day, he insisted, to hunt out that second car from the lizard valley and compare the two.

Dessie kept near them as they worked. She was Dard's shadow in the waking hours, as she had always been since taking her first uncertain steps. The other children were objects to be watched with sober interest, but as yet she preferred company she knew. And, since she was perfectly content to sit quietly, absorbed in the antics of the hoppers, insects, and the butterfly-birds, they often forgot she was with them.

"No——"

Dard was startled into turning by her sudden cry. She was having a tug of war with the largest hopper he had yet seen, a grandfather of a clan at least. But Dessie's strength was superior, and she wrenched away the prize the animal had just stolen from the blouse Dard had discarded in the heat.

"He opened your pocket," she told the boy indignantly, "and he took this out, just as if it were his own! What is it? Pretty——" She crooned the word as she fingered the sheets in which colors ran in waving bands.

"Why—I'd forgotten all about that. It's a book—or I think it is, Dessie. It belonged to Those Others."

"A *what!*" Kimber reached for it. "Where did you get it, kid?"

Dard explained how he had found it in the hidden room of the gun emplacement and of his theory that Those Others might have used the bands of color as a means of communication.

"I was going to compare it with those shots you took on microfilm of that doorway in the city. And then so much happened I forgot all about it."

"You do have a feeling for word patterns—I remember."

"Dard makes pictures out of words." Dessie answered for him. "Show how, Dardie."

Under Kimber's interested eyes Dard sketched out the pattern of a line of verse. The pilot nodded.

"Patterns for words. And that must be how you understood the importance of this. All right. Remember those rolls of some kind of recording tape we found in the first carrier? Rogan believes that they can be read by the help of our machines. You're going down to the ship right now and tell him to get out that equipment. We didn't see any use for it yet and it's been left down there. But I want to know—— Yes, go right now!"

So Dard, with Dessie still in tow, set off down river to the seashore where the remains of the star ship were being dismantled as fast as they could use its materials at the cliffs. The red spider plants were again floating in wide patches on the water, but not cloaking all the river as they had on the day the ship landed.

"I haven't been down here yet," Dessie confided. "Mrs. Harmon says that there are bad dragons."

Dard was quick to underline that warning. Dessie might just try to make friends with one of the things!

"Yes, there are, Dessie. And they are not like the animals at all. Promise me that if you see one you will call me right away!"

She was apparently impressed by his gravity for she agreed at once.

"Yes, Dardie. Mr. Rogan brought me a pretty shell from the sea. Might I just go down and see if I can find another?" Dessie asked.

"Stay in sight of the ship and don't wander away," he told her, seeing no reason why she should not hunt for treasures along the water's edge.

The ship which had been so solid and secure against the dangers of outer space was but a shell of her former self. In some places she had been stripped down to the inner framework. Dard squeezed through open partitions to a storeroom where he found the techneer checking the markings on a pile of boxes. When he explained his errand Rogan was enthusiastic.

"Sure we can try reading those tapes. We'll need this, and this, and"—he pushed aside a larger container to free a third—"this. I'll go to work assembling as soon as we get this back to the cliff. Might be able to try running off one roll tonight or early tomorrow. Want to give me a hand?"

Dard took one of the boxes under his arm and hooked his fingers in the carrying handle of another before tramping back over the ramp to the sand.

"Dessie came down with me. She wanted some more sea shells. I'll have to round her up."

"Sure thing." Rogan set down his large box and came along. They were almost at the shore when the scream sent them into a run.

"Dardie! Dardie! Quick——!"

Dard's hand went to the ray gun Cully had given him after the adventure with the lizards. It had a full charge in it now. But they had seen no trace of the monsters here!

"There she is! By those rocks!"

But he didn't need Rogan's direction. Dard had already sighted Dessie, her back to some sea-washed rocks, shying stones at one of the flying dragons, while she continued to shout for help. To Dard's surprise she made no move to join her rescuers but stood her ground valiantly until he used the ray to slice the head of the dragon and send its body flopping into the sea.

"Come here!" he called but she shook her head. He saw tears on her cheeks.

"It's the sea baby, Dardie, the little baby out of the sea. It's so afraid! We must help it——"

Dard stopped, catching at Rogan to bring him to a halt also. He trusted Dessie's instincts. She had been protecting another creature, not herself, and he had a feeling now that her act was of vast importance to them all. He schooled his voice to a low, even level as he said:

"All right, Dessie. The dragon is dead. Can you get the sea baby to come out now—or shall I come to help you?"

She smeared her hand across her wet face. "I can do it, Dard. It's so frightened and it might be more afraid of somebody as big as you."

She squatted down before a small opening between two rocks and made soft coaxing sounds. At last she turned her head.

"It's coming out. But you must stay away—please——"

Dard nodded. Dessie held out her hand to the hollow between the rocks. He was sure he saw something hesitatingly touch that small palm. Then she wriggled back, still coaxing.

What followed her brought a gasp from Dard, even inured as he now was to the surprises this world had to offer. Some twenty slender inches tall, it walked upright, the four tiny digits of one hand confidently hooked about Dessie's fingers. In color the creature was a soft silvery gray, but when a shaft of sunlight touched the fluff of thick fur which completely covered it, rainbow lights twinkled from each hair tip.

Its head was round, with no vestige of ears, the eyes very large, turning from Dessie to the two men. When it caught sight of them it stopped short and, with a gesture which won Dard completely, put the other hand to its wide, fanged mouth, chewing on its fingertips shyly. The small feet were webbed and scaled with rainbow tints, as were the hands. He continued to examine it, puzzled. It was akin to the night-howling monkeys, but it was much smaller and plainly amphibian. And it appeared to be able to see perfectly well in the daylight.

"Where did it come from, Dessie?" he asked quietly, trying hard not to alarm the engaging little thing.

"Out of the sea," she waved her free hand at the waves. "I was hunting shells and I found a pretty one. When I went down to wash the sand off it there he was, coming out of the water to watch me. He was sleeked down with the wet then—he's a lot prettier now——" She broke off and stopped to address her companion with a series of chirrups such as Dard had heard her use with the wild things of lost Terra.

"Then," she continued, "that bad dragon came and chased him into the rocks and I called you—like you told me to, Dardie, if I saw a dragon. They *are* bad. The sea baby was so frightened."

"Did it tell you so?" asked Rogan eagerly.

Perhaps it was the vibration of his deeper voice in the air which sent the sea creature crowding against Dessie, half hiding its face against her.

"Please, Mr. Rogan," she shook her head reprovingly.

"He's afraid when you talk. No, I don't think he talks like us. I just know what he feels—here," she touched a forefinger to her head. "He wanted to play with me so he came ashore. He's a nice baby—the nicest I ever, ever knew! Better than a fox or a bunny or even the big owl."

"Great Space! Look there—off the rocks!"

Dard's eyes followed the line of Rogan's pointing finger. Two sleek round heads bobbed out of the water, great unblinking orbs were turned to the party on the beach. Dard's grasp on Rogan's arm tightened.

"Keep quiet! This is important!"

Dessie beamed at their interruption.

"More sea people! Look, baby!" She directed the merchild's attention seaward.

Instantly it slipped its hand free and ran to the edge of the water. But, just as it was about to plunge into the waves, it stopped and looked back at Dessie. While it teetered there, toes in the lapping waves, the two others of its race swam into the shallows and arose to their feet to wade in. The merchild made up its mind and splashed out to meet the shorter of the two advancing figures and was gathered up in eager arms. The largest of the three—an inch or two above four feet Dard judged—moved in between its mate and child and those on shore.

"See what it's carrying!" Rogan schooled his voice with an effort.

But Dard needed no one to point out that discovery. The merman was armed with a spear, a spear with a mean looking many barbed head. And about his loins was a belt supporting a small, fastened case and a long dagger of pointed bone. This was no animal!

The merchild struggled to free itself, slipped under the reaching hand of its father, and darted back to Dessie. Grabbing again at her hand, it tugged her toward the couple in the water. Dard moved up, he didn't like the look of that spear.

But before he could get to Dessie the merman thrust that weapon at something washing along the rocks. When he raised the spear its point impaled the headless body of the dragon. With a gesture of fury the merman smashed the battered corpse down on the stone, ripping it off the barbs. Then he splashed up to Dessie and caught the mer-child, giving it a smart slap across its buttocks with a very human expression of exasperation. Dard chuckled and forgot his momentary fears.

The merpeople were unhuman in appearance but they appeared to share certain emotions with the Terrans. Dard stepped cautiously into the water. The merman was instantly alert, his spear on guard, backing toward his mate and the child he had pushed out to her.

Dard held out empty hands in the gesture of good will as old as time. The merman's big eyes searched his. Then slowly that spear was lowered, to be laid on wet sand, with webbed toes curled over it to hold it safe, and the rainbow scaled paws were raised in the right answer.

9.   TREATY AND ALLIANCE

"WHEN'S BLAST-OFF?" Cully was boring holes in the sand with one finger, restless away from his machines.

Dard glanced along the line of the six men who had accompanied him down to the shore. They sat cross-legged in the sand with strict orders to keep quiet and wait. The first meeting between the Terrans and the representatives of the merpeople had been scheduled for this afternoon—if he had been able to get the idea across in gestures alone.

Spread out on the shore several feet above the water level were those gifts the Terrans believed might please sea dwellers. Some nested plastic bowls made a bright-colored spot, a collection of empty bottles of various sizes, hastily assembled from laboratory supplies, golden apples, native grain, all there together. Objects which could be used under water had been hard to find.

"They're coming!" Dessie had been waiting impatiently by the waves' sweep, and now, heedless of the water curling about her legs, she ran forward, holding out her hands to the merchild who threshed up a fountain of spray in its eagerness to meet her. Hand in hand they pattered to dry land where the merchild shrank shyly against the little girl when it saw the men.

But Dessie was smiling and said importantly, "Ssssat and Ssssutu are coming now."

Dard hid his surprise. How could Dessie so confidently mouth those queer names—how did she *know?* From all his questioning—and Kimber's and Kordov's and Carlee's —last night, they had only been able to elicit that the "sea people thought into her head." They had been forced to accept the concept of telepathy—which could be possible with an undersea race.

So, deciding that Dessie's interpretation might be needed that day, they had schooled her in her part.

Ssssat and Ssssutu—if those were the proper designations of the mermen who were borne in with the next wave—came ashore. They both carried the barbed spears and wore long bone daggers at the belts which were their only articles of clothing. Without a sound they seated themselves on the seaside of the gifts, facing Dard, regarding him and the other Terrans with owlish solemnity.

"Dessie!" Dard called, and she came trotting to him.

"Do I give the presents now, Dard?"

"Yes. Try to make them understand that we want to be friends."

She picked out two of the bowls, put an apple and a handful of grain into each, and carried them over to set down before the envoys.

The one on Dard's right held out his hand and Dessie, without hesitation, laid hers, palm down, upon it. For a long moment they made contact. Then both mermen relaxed their tense watchfulness. They put their spears behind them and one ran his hands through the fur on his head and shoulders where it was fast drying into rainbow dotted fluff.

"They want to be friends, too," Dessie reported. "Dardie, if you put your hand on theirs, then they can talk to you. They don't talk with their mouths at all. This is Ssssat——"

Dard got to his feet slowly so as not to alarm the mermen and crossed the strip of shore until he could sit face to face. Then he held out his hand. Cool and damp the scaled digits and palm of the other lay upon his warmer flesh. And, Dard almost broke the contact in his surprise and awe, for the other *was* talking to him! Words, ideas, swept into his mind—some concepts so alien he could not understand. But bit by bit he pieced together much of what the other was striving to tell him.

"Big ones, land dwellers, we have watched you—with fear. Fear that you have come to lead us once more into the pens of darkness——"

"Pens of darkness?" Dard echoed aloud and then shaped a mental query.

"Those who once walked the land here—they kept the pens of darkness where our fathers' fathers' fathers' "—the concept of a long stretch of past time trailed through the Terran's receptive mind—"were hatched. The days of fire came and we broke forth and now we shall never return." There was stern warning, an implied threat, in that.

"We know nothing of the pens, nor do we threaten you," Dard thought slowly. "We, too, have broken out of pens of darkness," he added with sudden inspiration.

"It is true that you are not the color or shape of those who made the pens. And you have shown only friendship. Also you killed the flying death which would have slain my cub. I believe that you are good. Will you stay here?"

Dard pointed inland. "We build there."

"Do you wish the fruits of the river?" came next.

"The fruits of the river?" Dard was puzzled until a clear picture of one of the red spider plants formed in his mind. Then he shook his head to reinforce his unspoken denial.

"We may then come and harvest as we have always done? And," there was a shrewd bargaining note in this, "perhaps you will see that the flying death does not attack us, since your slaying powers are greater than ours?"

"We like the dragons no better than you do. Let me speak with the others now——" Dard broke contact and reported to the Terran committee.

"Sure!" Santee's jovial boom could not be kept to a whisper and at the sound, or its vibration, both mermen started. "Let 'em come in and get their spiders. I'll watch for dragons."

"Fair enough," Kimber agreed. "We don't care for the dragons any more than they do."

Before the hour had passed cordial relations had been established, and the mermen promised to return early the next morning with their harvest crew. Carrying the gifts they waded out into the sea, Ssssat's cub riding on his father's shoulder. The little one waved back at Dessie until all three disappeared under water.

"Those pens they spoke of," Kordov mused later that night when they discussed the meeting in an open convocation of all the voyagers. "They must have been imprisoned at one time by the city builders and escaped during or after the war. But surely they weren't domestic animals."

"More likely slaves," suggested Carlee Skort. "Perhaps they were forced to do undersea work where landsmen could not venture. They are coming tomorrow? Well, why can't we all go down and meet them? Maybe we can help in the harvesting and prove our good will."

The clamor which interrupted and supported her was indicative of the enthusiasm of the rest. Dessie's merpeople had caught the imaginations of all. And Dard believed that the Terrans would have gone to meet them in any case.

Early as the colonists came down to the river bank the next morning, the merpeople were there before them, wading along the shallows of the slowly flowing stream, sweeping between them woven basket nets, as fine as sieves, to skim up the red fungi. Merchildren paddled in and out, and a line of spear-bearing males patrolled the shoreline with attention for the cliff perches of the dragons.

They stopped all these activities as the Terrans came into sight, and when they began again it was with a certain self-consciousness. Dard and the others who had been on the seashore the day before went up to meet the sea people, their hands outstretched.

A party of the armed males split off to face them. In the center of their group was one portly individual who, though there was no way save by size for the humans to guess at merman ages, gave the impression of dignity and authority.

Dard touched palms with the leading warrior.

"This is Aaaatak, our 'Friend of Many.' He would communicate with your 'Giver of Law.'"

"Giver of Law." Kordov came the nearest to being the leader of the colonists. Dard beckoned to the First Scientist.

"This is their chieftain, sir. He wants to speak to our leader."

"So? I can not call myself leader," Kordov met the hands of the older merman, "but I am honored to speak to him." As Kordov and the merchief clasped hands the rest of the colonists came up, timidly. But an hour later merpeople and humans mingled with freedom. And when the Terran party set out food, the mermen brought in their own supplies, flat baskets of fish and aquatic plants, kept in water until time to eat. They accepted the golden apples eagerly, but kept away from the fires where their hosts cooked the fish they offered in return. Although each fire had a ring of amazed spectators, standing at a safe distance to gaze at the wonder.

Three dragons that dared to invade were brought down with rays, to the savage exultation of the merpeople. They asked to inspect the weapons and returned them regretfully when they understood that such arms would not last in their water world.

"Though," Cully said thoughtfully, when this had been explained, "I don't see why they couldn't use some of the metal forged by Those Others. It seems to resist rust and erosion on land—it might in the water."

"Nordis!"

The urgency in that call brought Dard away from the engineer to the small group of Kimber, Kordov, the merchief and several others. Harmon was there, as well as Santee, and some techneers.

"Yes, sir?"

"You've seen the lizards, ask Aaaatak if those are what he is trying to tell us about. We can't get the right impression of what he means and it seems to be vitally important." Kordov edged back for the boy to take his place. Dard clasped the readily extended claws of the merchief.

"Do you wish to tell us about——" He shut his eyes in order to concentrate better upon a mental image of the huge reptiles.

"No!" The answer was a decided negative. "Those we have seen, yes—hunting down other land dwellers. They were once subordinate to those we speak of now. These——"

Another picture indeed—a biped—humanoid in outline —but somehow all wrong. Dard had seen nothing like it. And the image was fuzzy, indistinct as if he observed it from a distance—or through water!

Through water! That was caught up eagerly by Aaaatak.

"Now you are thinking straight. We do not come out of hiding when those are about! So we see them in that fashion——"

"They live on land, then? Near here?" Dard demanded. The emotion of fear colored so strongly all the impressions he received from the merchief.

"They live on land, yes. Near here, no, or we should not be here. We hunt out shores where they do not come. Once they were very, very many, living everywhere—here— across the sea. They were the builders of those pens where creatures of my kind were imprisoned for them to work their will upon. Then something happened. There came fire raining from the sky, and a sickness which struck them. They died, some quickly, some much more slowly, when my people burst from the pens." There was a cold and deadly satisfaction in that flash of memory. "After that we fled into the wilds of the sea where they could not find us. Even when I was but a new-hatched cub we lived in the depths. But through the years our young warriors went out to search for food and for a safer place to live—there are monsters in the deeps as horrible as the lizards of the land. And these parties discovered that those"—again Dard saw the queer biped—"were gone from long stretches among the reefs, as we had always longed to do.

"There are none of those left in this land now but——" The merchief hesitated before suddenly withdrawing his hand from Dard's and turning to his followers as if consulting them. Dard took the opportunity to translate to the others what he had learned.

"Survivors of Those Others," Kimber caught him up. "But not here?"

"No. Aaaatak says that his people will not come where they are. Wait—he has more to tell."

For Aaaatak was holding out his hand and Dard met it readily.

"My people now believe that you are not like those. You do not seem in body quite the same, your skin is of a different color," he drew his claw finger across the back of Dard's hand to emphasize his meaning, "and you have received us as one free people greets another. This those others do not—there is much hate and bitterness between us from the far past—and they always delight in killing.

"We have watched you ever since you first came out of the sky. Those others once traveled in the sky—though of late we have not seen their bird ships—and so we thought you of the same breed. Now we know that that is untrue. But we must tell you—be on your guard! For on the other side of the sea those others still live, even if their numbers are few, and there is a blackness in their minds which leads them to raise spears against all living things!

"Now," Dard had a strong impression that the merchief was coming to the main point, "we are a people who know much about the sea, but little of the land. We have learned that you are not native of this world, having fallen from the sky—but, did you not also say that you came from a place where you, too, were penned by enemies?"

Dard assented, remembering his statement to the firs
envoys.

"If you are wise you will not seek out those who woul
lay such bonds upon you again. For that is what thos
others will do. In this world they recognize no other right
or desires than are born of their own wills. We have war
riors of our race who keep watch upon them secretly an
bring news of their coming and going. Against their might—
though they have lost much of their ancient knowledge—
we have only our own cunning and knowledge of the sea
And what good is a spear against that which may kill a
a distance? But you have mightier weapons. And shoul
we two peoples join skills and hearts against *them*—— Bu
do you now say this to your Giver of Laws and othe
Elder Ones so that they may understand." He withdrew hi
hand again and left Dard to interpret.

"An alliance!" Tas Kordov caught the meaning of tha
offer. "Hmm," he plucked his lower lip. "Better tell him—
No, let me. I'll explain that we shall talk it over."

"What's all this 'bout Those Others?" Harmon demanded
"Did they," he indicated the merpeople, "say that they'r
still here—the ones who lived in that city?"

"Not here—across the sea," Dard was beginning whe
Rogan broke in.

"That chieftain doesn't think much of them, does he?"

"He says they're enemies."

"They aren't his kind," Harmon pointed out. "And hi
people were their slaves once."

"We," Kimber said slowly, "have had some experienc
with slavery ourselves, haven't we? On Terra we'd hav
been in labor camps, if we hadn't been lucky—that is if w
weren't shot down in cold blood. I have a pretty good mem
ory of the last few years there."

Harmon sifted a palmful of sand from one hand to an
other. "Yeah, I know. Only we don't want to get into n
local war."

That echoed after his voice died away. No entanglin
alliances to drag them into any war! Dard sensed the electri
agreement which ran through them at that thought. Onl

Kimber, Santee, and maybe Kordov, did not wholly agree with Harmon.

Dard gazed down to the river bank. The merpeople had almost completed the harvest and were gathering up their possessions and slipping in family groups back to the sea. He wondered what Kordov would tell the chief.

Suddenly he could not stand the uncertainty any longer. He wanted to get away—to escape from the thought that perhaps it was going to start all over again—the insecurity—the constant guard duty against a hostile force.

According to the merchief Those Others were now across the sea—but would they remain there? Wouldn't this fertile, deserted land where they had once ruled draw them back again? And they would not accept new settlers kindly.

If the Terrans only knew more about them! Those Others had blasted their world. Dard remembered the callous cruelty of that barn in the valley. Raids, looting, the blasted city, the robot-controlled guns to shoot anything passing out of the air, the warnings of the merpeople.

He plodded across the sand to the inner valley, heading for the cliff house. Rogan had set up the projector the night before, and they had put the first of the discovered tapes in it. If something about the rulers of this world could be learned from those—this was the time to do it!

"Where're you bound for, kid?" Kimber fell into step.

"The cliffs." Dard was being pushed by the feeling that time was not his to waste, that he must know—now!

The pilot asked no more questions but followed Dard into the rock cell where Rogan had installed his machine. The boy checked the preparation made the night before. He turned off the light—the screen on the wall was a glowing square of blue-white and then the projector began to hum.

"This one of those rolls from the carrier?"

But Dard did not answer. For now the screen was in use. He began to watch. . . .

"Turn it off! Turn that off!"

His frenzied fingers found the proper button. They were surrounded by honest light, clean red-yellow walls.

Kimber's face was in his hands, the harshness of his breathing filled the room. Dard, shaken, sick, dared not move. He gripped the edge of the shelf which supported the projector, gripped so tightly that the flesh under his nails turned dead white. He tried to concentrate upon that phenomenon—not on what he had just seen.

"What—what did you see?" he moistened his lips and asked dully. He had to know. Maybe it was only his own reaction. But—but it couldn't be! The very thought that only he had seen *that* led to panic—to a terror beyond bearing.

"I don't know . . ." Kimber's answer dragged out of him word by painful word. "It wasn't meant—ever meant for man—our kind of man—to see——"

Dard raised his head, made himself stare at that innocuous screen, to assure himself that there was nothing there now.

"It did something to me—inside," he half whispered.

"It was meant to, I think. But—Great Lord—what sort of minds—feelings—did they have! Not human—totally alien. We have no common meeting point—we never shall have—with that!"

"And it was all just color, twisting, turning color," Dard began.

Kimber's hand closed about his wrist with crushing intensity.

"I was right," Dard did not feel the pain of that grip, "they used color as a means of communication. But—but——"

"What they had to say with it! Yes, not for us—never for us. Keep your mind off it, Dard. Five minutes more of that and you might not have been human—ever again!"

"We couldn't establish contact with them—with——"

"Minds that could conceive that? No, we can't. So that was what brought you here—you wanted to see if Harmon was right in his neutral policy? Now you know—with that we have no common ground. And we'll have to make the others understand. If we do meet Those Others—the result will undoubtedly be war."

"Fifty-three of us—maybe a whole nation of them left."

Dard was still sick and shaken—sensing a deep inner violation.

First there had been the tyranny of Pax, which had been man-made and so understandable, in all its narrow cruelty, because it had been the work of human beings. And now this—which man dared not—touch!

Kimber had regained control of himself. There was even a trace of the familiar impish grin on his face as he said:

"When the fighting is the toughest, that's when our breed digs in toes. And we needn't borrow trouble. Get Kordov and Harmon in here. If we are going to discuss the offer of the mermen we want them to know what to expect from overseas."

But—to Dard's dismay—the projection of Those Others' tapes aroused in Harmon no more than a vague uneasiness —though it shook Kordov. And, as they insisted on the rest of the men viewing it, they discovered that it varied in its effects upon different individuals. Rogan, sensitive to communication devices, almost fainted after a few moments' strict attention. Santee admitted that he did not like it but couldn't say why. But, in the end, the weight of evidence was that they could not hope to deal with Those Others.

"I'm still sayin'," Harmon insisted, "that we shouldn't get pulled into anything them seapeople has started. You say them pictures make Those Others regular devils. Well, they're still across the sea. We shouldn't go lookin' for trouble—then maybe we don't find none!"

"We're not suggesting an expeditionary force, Tim," Kimber answered mildly. "But if they are alive overseas they may just get the idea to reclaim this land—and you'd want to know about it ahead of time if they did. The mermen will keep us informed. Then we could supply them with better arms."

"Yeah, and right there you've got trouble! You make sea-goin' ray guns and the first thing you know they're gonna use 'em. They hate Those Others, don't they? Back on earth we picked off a Peaceman whenever we got the chance, didn't we? And let that happen a coupla times and Those Others are gonna come lookin' for where those new guns came from. I ain't sayin' we oughta turn our backs on the mermen—they seem peaceful. But we're plain foolish if we get mixed up in any war of theirs. I said it before and I'm gonna keep on sayin' it!"

"All right, Tim. And you're speaking the truth. But this is good land, ain't it?"

"Sure, it's good land! We're gonna have a mighty fine farm here. But farmin' and fightin' don't mix. What about that fella what lived right over there? He didn't live out the last war, did he?"

"Suppose they want this good land back? How long can we defend it?"

For the first time a shadow of doubt appeared in Tim Harmon's eyes.

"Okay!" he flung up a hand in surrender. "I'll go with you halfway. I say be friends with the mermen and help 'em—some. But I'm not gonna vote for no gangin' up with 'em in a private war!"

"That's all we want you to do, Tim. We'll ally with the mermen and make plans for defense," Kordov soothed him.

Dard smiled wryly. Inside he was amused, amused and tired. They had come across the galaxy to escape to freedom, only to live again under the shadow of fear. It was a long way to travel to come—home!

A new frontier to guard. What was that thing Kimber had once quoted while standing on a mountainside in the Terran winter?

"Frontiers of any type, physical or mental, are but a challenge to our breed. Nothing can stop the questing of men, not even Man. If we will it, not only the wonders of space, but the very stars are ours!"

They had known the wonders of space, the stars were theirs—if they could hold them! But who—or what—dared to say that they could not? Why, Dard savored the new pride growing hotly within him, they had broken the bonds of space——

There was a wide world before them, unlimited in its possibilities. On distant Terra this ill-assorted group had drawn into tight alliance because they believed alike—in

what? Freedom—Man's freedom! They had faced the steril-
ity of Pax clear-eyed and refused to be bound by it—
entrusting their lives to the knowledge Pax had outlawed—
and it had brought them here. They—if they willed it—
worked for a united goal—they could do anything!

Dard's eyes were on the painted cliffs but inwardly he
saw beyond—across the wide and waiting land. Alliance
with the merpeople—taming of the land—building a new
civilization—his breath came faster. Why, a lifetime was not
going to be time enough to do everything that even he could
see had to be done.

Could their breed be defeated? He gave his answer to
the uncertain future with a single word:

"NO!"